Mary Graham

Fanny Percy's Knight-Errant

Mary Graham

Fanny Percy's Knight-Errant

ISBN/EAN: 9783337280703

Printed in Europe, USA, Canada, Australia, Japan

Cover: Foto ©Andreas Hilbeck / pixelio.de

More available books at **www.hansebooks.com**

KNIGHT-ERRANT.

BY THE AUTHOR OF

" THE WHOLE ARMOR," " GERTRUDE TERRY," ETC.

How far a little candle throws its Beams !"

The National Temperance Society and Publication House,

 READE STREET.

1876.

CONTENTS.

CHAPTER VII.

CHAPTER VIII.

CHAPTER IX.

CHAPTER X.

CHAPTER XI.

CHAPTER XII.

CHAPTER XIII.

CHAPTER XIV.

FANNY PERCY'S KNIGHT-ERRANT.

CHAPTER I.

LAST DAYS AT HOME.

ANNY! let me hear you say once more, 'I forgive.'" The dying man looked into his daughter's eyes, to read there the words which she had said so often, and which he never seemed tired of hearing.

How was it that she could forget the weary, toilsome years which had made

her old before even the sweet spring-
tide of youth had come to her? Hers
had been a hard life thus far, and it
might have been so pleasant, so happy,
but for the foe which had been in their
household almost since she could remember, and which had made her father oh!
so different from what he once had been.
For, yes, now that love was drawing a
veil over those last dark years, it seemed
as if a faint light were thrown upon
the early days of her childhood, when
father, mother, sisters, and brothers had
lived so happily together in that beautiful country place which had been sold
from them so long ago; she could not,
would not think of all that had inter-

vened since then—how, one after another, the dear ones had been taken
away, and she alone of all those children
left to drink to the full the cup of sorrow, whose capacity seemed deepening
every year.

For from the time of his wife's death
Mr. Percy had given himself up unrestrainedly to what had at first been only
an occasional temptation. Her sweet,
gentle influence had not been all in
vain, but when it was removed there
seemed no other way of "drowning
thought," as he expressed it, except in
the wine-cup. Oh! that he had learnt,
before sorrow came, to look to the only
Source of strength. Then he would

have found that any trial, any affliction, can be borne with Jesus to share the load. But, alas! he had listened rather to that other voice, which lured him away from the right under a false promise of comfort. For comfort he had needed sorely; his was naturally an affectionate disposition, and he had deeply felt the loss of the dear help-mate on whom he had been wont to lean, and who had used her utmost efforts to keep temptation out of his way.

The sequel is of almost too common occurrence to need to be told: step by step the downward path was taken, until not a day passed that did not find him stupefied by liquor. His accustomed tasks had one by one to be relinquished, and the support of the family had gradually devolved upon the eldest children, with such help as was occasionally sent by his wife's far-away brother.

At intervals he would seem to awaken to a sense of his unlooked-for degradation, and then such pangs of remorse would overtake him that the most unsympathizing could hardly have failed to pity him.

And now the end was drawing near— not from delirium tremens, which had been often prophesied for him, but by the fell destroyer consumption, less swift, perhaps, but not less sure when once it sets its mark on its victim. Fanny was the only one of all his dear ones left to minister to him in these last days of suffering and remorse. The neighbors came in and were kind and attentive, as poor people are apt to be in times of distress. They recognized the fact that Mr. Percy had once been a gentleman, and their hearts warmed with pity for the poor young girl "who might have sat with the best ladies in the land."

About a month before a kind clergyman had called, and had poured some drops of comfort upon those two wounded hearts. Mr. Percy had listened to him respectfully, and even submissively, but it was hard to tell whether any great

change was wrought in his soul by
means of these kind ministrations. Who
shall judge a dying man, or which of
us shall say that his prayer of repentance may not be heard? Our own duty
is to attend to these things, to have our
lamps trimmed and our lights burning
before the messenger of the bridegroom
cometh; but this dying man could only
think of one whose repentance was received even as he was dying upon the
cross, and of one other who could not
so much as lift up his eyes to heaven,
but smote upon his breast, saying, "God
be merciful to me a sinner!"

His chief remorse was for the dear
child who had been faithful to him

through everything. He could look back
now with sharp pain upon those years
which should have been the most bright
and joyous of her life, but which had
been darkened by his drunken neglect.
An added thrill of pain came to him
as he thought of her education, or rather
the want of it. How he would once
have enjoyed developing that intellect,
which even these most unpropitious sur-
roundings had not succeeded in render-
ing dull! for somehow Fanny had made
the very most of her few opportunities,
and her mind had grown and thriven on
the few books which still remained of
her father's once fine library. These she
had read and re-read, and had perhaps

derived more mental nourishment there-from than she might have done from a larger number lightly skimmed over.

Her father had talked more with her in the last month than he had ever done before; and although their topics of conversation were various, and he was astonished at the stock of intelli-gence she had contrived to lay in from such meagre sources, they always drifted back to the one theme most interesting to the dying man.

Again and again did Fanny have to assure him of her forgiveness, and she would fain have pointed him to the one true Source of pardon and peace; but as yet she herself was but as one groping in the dark, and how could she show him the way? She could but read such portions from her mother's little Bible as seemed most suitable, hardly realizing that while she was pouring balm into her father's soul the good seed was being planted in her own hitherto neglected heart.

Once she tried to ask in turn for forgiveness on her part; for had she not often been impatient and complaining, and had not, perhaps, made the home as pleasant and attractive as it ought to have been? But her father would not listen to her self-reproaches.

"You've been a brave, good girl, and I wonder you did not leave me long ago when your cousins wrote to you to come."

"O father! don't. How could I?"

'How could you stay with such a wretch as I have been; but you've forgiven me, and perhaps after I am gone you can have a happy life after all." Then, after a tearful silence:

"I need hardly ask you to make me one promise. Fanny."

"What is it, dear father?"

"Never, under any circumstances, to take a glass of intoxicating liquor—not even home-made wine. Remember, not even home-made wine."

Fanny gave the promise solemnly, and her father continued:

"Above all, Fanny, never offer it to any one else; you never, *never* can tell what the result may be. It was that that first upset me. Oh! if I had never touched the first glass; and how many can say the same thing! Promise me now on your word -and honor!

Fanny needed no persuasion; she had too great a horror of intemperance to incline her to any lenience towards "moderate drinking," but she had no idea that this solemn promise would be of real service to her in the future.

Into that future she dared not look; her father, his comfort and peace, was all that she thought of just now. If "prayer is the soul's sincere desire," then did she have many a prayer for his well-being; but as yet she had not learned to carry her sorrows to One who is "a very present help in time of trouble." She had not learned to view these very sorrows as so many evidences of the chastening hand which chasteneth because He loveth. Some time, perhaps, she will recognize the love which traced itself through the darkest cloud of her life; but now it is rather as with the stern Judge than the loving Father or Saviour that she tries to hold communion with her God.

Those last days with her earthly father—can she ever draw a veil over

them? Can she ever forget the long
days and longer nights of anguish.
mingled now and then with some few
drops of comfort which she treasures
up for years afterwards?

"Though your sins be as scarlet,
they shall be as white as snow: though
they be red like crimson, they shall be
as wool"; these were the last words
she read to him on the night when
death's messenger came.

"Though your sins be as scarlet,
they shall be as white as snow."
Over and over again she repeated this
to herself as her uncle led her from
the room; then the thought came to
her, "Her work on earth was over;

what was there left for her to do but to follow him whom she had loved so tenderly and faithfully?"

But God had other work for her to do that she knew not of. He alone could send the preparation needed for that work, and no doubt all that she had passed through had had no small part in fitting her for what lay before her.

Many a time there seems to come a "great wind from the wilderness," smiting and taking from us what the heart holds most dear. Who can fill the vacuum caused by the death of our dearest one? What work can take the place of our tender devotion to him?

There remaineth ever One for whom we may work so long as life endureth. Our work may be the active service, or it may be, if he so wills it, the "patient waiting" so much harder to bear; but work there is, and ever will be, in the great cause in which every true Christian should be an enlisted soldier.

CHAPTER II.

 UCH an old-fashioned little thing!" exclaimed Clara Lodor as Fanny passed up to her room, having just been inspected and welcomed, after a fashion, by her aunt and cousins.

"How old did you say she is, father? I could not tell whether she was a little girl or a lady of 'uncertain age,'" said Matilda, the eldest daughter.

"About sixteen, I think."

"Just my age!" exclaimed school-boy

John; "then we'll be twins, won't we? That's just jolly. She must have been a regular brick to have stuck to her father that way."

"John! Such language!" exclaimed Matilda, with an upward curl of her very expressive nose; then, turning to her father, added: "I am real sorry the children happened to hear anything about our aunt's husband; it will be sure to get out among some of our friends about him and the way they have been living."

"John, you must not mention it, and tell Nettie also—that is, if she knows anything about it. It would never do in the world if that should leak out; and, girls, I want you all to be as kind to Fanny as you know how. Put some of your style into her, if you can." And he gave an admiring glance at the fashionable appearance of his wife and daughters.

"She will only be a school-girl, won't she?" said Clara, who had been half-relieved to find that their cousin would not be a possible rival for her; there was nothing more awkward, she thought, than to have two or three "come-out" young ladies under the same roof.

"I will leave all that to you, Henrietta," returned Mr. Lodor, turning to his wife. He could not imagine

Fanny's being turned into a little, silly school-girl (for such he generally considered them to be)—she whom he had seen taking a woman's part for the last week, who had shown more strength, tact, and endurance than many a woman of twice her age might have possessed

"Oh! it will be much better for her to go to school for a year or two," replied Mrs. Lodor, who had decided upon this some time ago as the easiest way of disposing of their charge. She had made no objections when her husband had written, saying that he would bring his niece home with him as soon as possible after the funeral. It was the only thing to be done, and Mrs. Lodor had accepted it, not as a labor of love nor as a service rendered unto her Lord, but as a thing inevitable, which could not be got out of. She was not altogether without religious feelings and motives, but they occupied a very subordinate part in her life. Perhaps her life hitherto had been too smooth and easy to make her feel the need of that "refuge and strength" which religion alone can give; at any rate it was far from being brought into her daily actions as the ruling guide and motive.

To do well by her children, to see them prosperous, gay, and happy, and,

when the time for each came, to have
them well settled in life—this was the
mainspring of life just now.   If Fanny
could take an unobtrusive place in her
household, without causing any distur-
bance of her plans and arrangements,
she would be perfectly welcome; and the
meanness which would have begrudged
the additional expense was fortunately
not one of her characteristics.

And so Fanny found herself domiciled
in the new home which was so different from the one she had left.   It was
lavish with every luxury that heart can
desire, and Fanny had her due share
in the ease and comfort so new, so
strange to her; and yet, and yet many

a time did her heart sigh for the olden time which seemed to be fading gradually away before the outward brightness of this new life. Even when she had become entirely accustomed to the luxury, the ease, and that entire absence of care and worriment which at first had been so hard to realize, she found deep down in her heart an unsatisfied feeling. She had tasted too deeply of the bitterness and sorrow of life to be easily contented with a mere outward show of happiness. Her soul seemed to be searching around for some strong foundation on which to rest, some safe, abiding source of happiness. Would no kindly hand point her to the way of life?

Her aunt had selected a less fashionable school than one of her own
children would have attended; for she
knew that Fanny's education had been
much neglected, and considered it better
to send her where the rudiments were
well and thoroughly taught. And now
the girl's studies formed the greatest
pleasure, as well as the greatest task,
of her life. Her thirst for knowledge
was insatiable, and her teachers sometimes feared she might be overtasking
herself. It was a real pleasure to them
to assist in the unfolding of that intellect, and perhaps they resisted too little
the temptation to spur it on to still
more rapid strides. Her pale cheeks

began to grow still more pale, and there was an undue excitement in her every movement which showed that her vital tissues were being wasted faster than nature could repair them.

Mrs. Lodor was as kind and attentive to her as her various avocations would permit, but that real tenderness was wanting which would have known at once that something was amiss. Matilda and Clara were too much wrapped up in their gayeties to give a second thought to the pale little thing who was never seen without a book in her hand. John and Nettie were the only ones with whom there was any semblance of friendship, and they

were too young to know what that
unnatural excitement, that hectic flush,
portended.

Mrs. Lambert, the assistant principal
of the school, was the only one that
felt any anxiety on Fanny's account.
She had been interested in her from
the first, and at first, like the other
teachers, had given way to the temptation of "pushing her on"; but now she
began to fear for the consequences, and
tried to make the other teachers appre-
ciate the necessity of abridging rather
than lengthening the tasks of the worn-
out girl.   Had she known all that
Fanny had been through before coming
to the school, it would have been no

matter of surprise to her that her over-wrought constitution was not equal to the burden imposed upon it; as it was, she could only take it for granted that she was overtaxing herself, and that it was the duty of the teachers to reduce her lessons.

As yet she had not succeeded in convincing them of the necessity; the temptation was too great, and their enthusiasm in watching the rapid development of the mental powers of their brightest scholar was not to be brooked by the consideration of her well-being.

One day there had been an unusually exciting contest in the geometry class. Fanny was at the black-board proving a proposition over which every other girl had stumbled, when, just as she had come to a triumphant conclusion, a sudden weakness overcame her, and she would have fallen to the floor but for Miss Coleman's hand stretched out to save her. Restoratives were applied, and she soon felt nearly as well as usual, but it was decided that she should do nothing more that day. She begged hard to be allowed to remain for mythology, but, as Mrs. Lambert had charge of that class, it was gently but decidedly refused.

"You had better go home just as soon as you feel strong enough," said Mrs. Lambert, who knew that the fresh air

would be the best thing for her. " I will
send Jennie Clark with you." And she
gave Fanny a kiss on the forehead which
seemed to do her more good than all the
hartshorn, salts, cologne, etc., which had
been placed at her service that morning.

The walk revived Fanny very much,
and by the time the two girls reached
home she was almost ashamed to tell
her aunt that she had come home ear-
lier than usual on account of sickness.
But faithful Jennie insisted upon coming
in and delivering verbatim the message
which Mrs. Lambert had sent: that
Fanny was to study no more that day,
and on no account to be sent to school
until she was perfectly well again.

"You do look a little pale; do you feel weak, child?" said Mrs. Lodor as soon as Jennie had delivered her message and gone; it would be very inconvenient to have a sick girl upon her hands with the dressmakers in the house and several parties coming off within the next week.

"Not very," said Fanny, trying to smile cheerfully. She did hope she would not have to stay away from school the next day, she was making such progress in her studies; and then that kiss on her forehead had brought her love for Mrs. Lambert to a kind of climax, and it seemed so long even for to-morrow to come, when she might see her again.

"You had better go up to the nursery

and lie down, and I will send you something strengthening." And Mrs. Lodor hurried from the room, as if to hasten from the very idea of what had been so repugnant to her. Fanny went up, as desired, to the room which still retained the name of "nursery," though rather by virtue of its old office than from its being used as such now. She threw herself down on the lounge, and was soon in a refreshing slumber; she knew not how long she had slept, when a creaking kind of sound aroused her, and, slowly opening her eyes, she could not but laugh as she caught sight of John walking on tip-toe to the door. He was trying hard to walk softly, but the more he tried the louder his boots creaked, and he turned around a little discomfited as he heard Fanny's low, soft laugh.

"Halloo! are you awake?" coming towards her, and nearly upsetting a waiter which was on a chair by her side. "Mother sent this up to you, and wants to know if you feel better; would have sent it before, but had to see about the 'fit' of Clara's dress."

Fanny glanced at the waiter which he held towards her, and a painful flush spread over her face as she saw the glass of wine which stood amidst several plates containing biscuits, bread and butter, etc.

"She said you'd better drink this, if

you feel weak." And John handed her the glass of wine; but Fanny rigidly locked her hands together, and a deadly paleness took the place of her former excited flush. All the painful past seemed brought back to her at sight of that glass of wine, and the solemn promise which she had made came to her with such overwhelming force that she turned dizzy at the very thought of its even being offered to her.

"O John! take it away. I cannot bear the sight of it."

"You don't know what's good. Mother'll be awfully put out; so, as I don't often get such a good chance, I'll—"

But Fanny jumped up with nervous

energy and dashed the glass from his hand in an almost frantic manner just as he had raised it to his lips.

" What in the name of senses is the matter with you ? " said John, as he wiped the wine from his clothes, and then attempted to gather up the broken fragments of glass which were scattered on the floor.

Fanny was too much excited to lie down again, but hurried over to the window for some air. " He had not taken it," was her thought; "and, oh! if he had it would have been her fault." A choking sensation overcame her, and by the time John had reached her side again a stream of blood was issuing from her mouth.

CHAPTER III.

FANNY FINDS TRUE JOY.

 EVERAL weeks have pass-ed away, and Fanny finds herself slowly recovering from the immediate effects of that exciting day. The dictum has gone forth which has caused her much sorrow and distress: "No more study, no more school," say the doctors, or it will be at the risk of Miss Per-cy's life. A little forethought, a mother's watchful care, might have prevented the necessity for this decision, but things

had been allowed to run on until that alarming climax had come which had startled the whole household into prudence.

It was a terrible cross to Fanny thus to be deprived of those pursuits which had been so fascinating, the more so as she had not as yet laid firm hold of that which only can fill up every vacuum in life; but God's ways are not as our ways, and we shall see how this very trial was one of the means used in bringing Fanny to the knowledge of that love which alone is all-satisfying.

Her school friends and teachers had sent many enquiries and kind messages, but as yet none of them had been allowed

to see her, as at first the slightest excitement might have proved fatal. Now,
however, she was able to sit up once
more, and was looking forward with an
indefinable pleasure to a visit from Mrs.
Lambert. It was a kind of marvel even
to herself how her heart-strings had
wound themselves so closely around her
new-found friend; for in general this lady
was rather cold and reserved among the
school-girls, and, though remarkably conscientious in the discharge of her duties, she seemed to keep the girls at a
distance. But something had drawn her
to Fanny from the first—perhaps an
intuitive feeling that she had sounded
deeper depths than most girls of her

age; and as she herself had long ago
found peace, even while passing under
the deepest waves of suffering, she had
a longing to carry the message of peace
to this younger disciple in affliction.

Some few little seeds of heavenly wisdom and comfort she had already drop-
ped into Fanny's heart, and these had
been growing steadily all through her
illness; for the first time she seemed to
think of her Saviour as a dear, loving
friend and brother, to whom she could
carry every trial, and whose ear would
ever be open unto her cry.

And now that she was recovering, she
began to realize that there must be
some work for her to do for the Sa-

viour; she longed to be enlisted in his
cause, and to feel that she was fighting
his battles.

To Mrs. Lambert alone could she
speak of what was going on in her
soul, and it was particularly for this
reason that she was looking forward so
anxiously for her first visit. She had
sent her a special message that she
would like to see her, and felt sure she
would come on that afternoon, if possible.

She had made up her mind to tell
her all her doubts and perplexities, her
wishes and longings, and this would be
at first a great effort; for hers was
rather a reserved nature. and, as she

had never had any one to whom to confide her deepest aspirations, it would be
doubly hard for her.

The front-door bell had rung for the
tenth time, and as many times had
Fanny's heart seemed to leap into her
mouth, but this time for some reason; for
did she not hear Mrs. Lambert's voice,
and was not that her firm yet gentle
footstep on the stairs? Her excitement
seemed hushed to rest as she found
herself folded in her friend's embrace,
and then, after a few minutes of quiet,
peaceful happiness, she lay down again
on the sofa, keeping hold of her friend's
hand.

"I have so much to say to you; you

don't know all that I have been thinking of since I saw you."

"Perhaps you had better let me do the
talking to-day," replied the other gently.

"Well, only let it be about — you
know. Do you remember our last talk—
so sweet!—about—"

"Our blessed Saviour?" And the
tear which started to Fanny's eye at
the sound of that dear name told her
teacher she had guessed right.

"Oh! yes; tell me more about him.
Is it really true that he will listen to
our prayers?"

"Fanny, when you sent for me to-day
you felt certain I would come, if possible,
did you not?"

"Oh! yes, ma'am."

"And how much more will He come than a mere earthly friend! With him 'nothing is impossible,' and he himself hath said, 'Ask, and ye shall receive; seek, and ye shall find; knock, and it shall be opened unto you.'"

"Oh! that is so sweet; tell me some more." And Mrs. Lambert talked or read on, in a like soothing strain, until Fanny's heart was so filled that the very name of Jesus seemed to bring peace and comfort with it.

"You have told me what he has done for me; now, the next time you must tell me what I can do for him,' she said as Mrs. Lambert stooped to bid her good-by ; and from that time her heart was filled more and more with a burning desire to do something for Him who had done everything, even to laying down his life, for her.

Could she lay down her life in his cause, or must she linger on day after day, weak and delicate, and fit for nothing but to try and bear this cross, which sometimes seemed so heavy? For she was trying to believe Mrs. Lambert when she told her that even such an apparently idle life might be consecrated to his use; that depression and pain, and even an unavoidable inactivity, if patiently borne for his sake, might ofttimes be acceptable fruit to this so kind husbandman. "They also serve who only stand and wait." These words came to her again and again, comforting her with the thought that even she, poor useless thing that she felt herself to be, might be truly serving as well as those who were able to enter into more active service.

Gradually there were things revealed to her which, while they filled her with sorrow, showed her that there might be work for her to do, even in this secluded sphere. As the duties of a Christian life gradually unfolded themselves to her, she could not but be painfully jarred by the so different standard by which her uncle's household was ruled; pleasure, convenience, comfort, seemed to be the rule of conduct, rather than the sense of duty which would have put these all to one side in the cause of right. There was one thing to which she most determinedly shut her eyes, until it was impossible to be any longer deceived by the statement which had long satisfied the world and which had been intended to satisfy her. Her uncle's frequent sicknesses, coming as they did once or twice a week, sometimes oftener—oh! that she might only hope on, as at first, that they were genuine illnesses. But no, she had had unmistakable evidence of their cause; it was the same as had brought her father to poverty and shame, only thus far Mrs. Lodor had been able to shield the fact of her husband's dissipation from general knowledge.

Fanny was almost overwhelmed with sorrow when the discovery forced itself upon her. She knew not which way to turn; her uncle, she knew, would merely laugh at any solicitations she might make to him to try and break his dreadful habit, and her aunt would probably be very angry if she said anything to her about it. Her pride was in keeping it from the world, and, though some must necessarily know it, at least they need say nothing to her about it. No, the time to speak had not yet come; it would do more harm than good, she felt, and she could only carry this new trouble to the Throne where she had learned to cast all care and sorrow.

But she need not be altogether useless in the good cause; a happy thought struck her one day, and she determined to put it into execution on the first opportunity. It would be out of her province to preach to those so much older than herself, and who ought to have been so much wiser, but at least she could make an effort to enlist her equals in the great cause which she had espoused.

CHAPTER IV.

FIRST EFFORTS IN THE CAUSE.

URING the first part of her sickness John had been very kind and attentive to her, seeming anxious to make amends for any part he might have had in bringing her disease to a crisis. In her recovery he had read to her, talked to her, and diverted her in every way that a boy could think of; but of late he had rather withdrawn from her, and seemed more engrossed in entertaining Harry Smith, a friend whom he had made at school, and from whom he seemed to have become inseparable.

Fanny had met this young gentleman once or twice, and was not at all impressed in his favor; he was a great deal older than John, and some instinct told her that his influence over her cousin would be anything but good. The moral atmosphere—what a subtle, almost imperceptible thing it is, and how often does a woman's instinct tell her more about it than any amount of fact or reasoning would do!

Every time these two had been together Fanny could have told it by the change in her cousin, even if his friend's name had not been mentioned;

and when by any chance they were separated for a few days, that malign influence, as Fanny could not help calling it in her heart, would wear off and he would be his own frank, kind self again.

It was on one of these occasions that she found the opportunity of saying what it had long been on her mind to say to John. But how should she introduce the subject? There was, she knew, such a thing as disgusting people even by an over-zeal in a good cause, and John was one of those who professed to hate "cant, and saints, and all that nonsense."

But should she see him gradually drifting towards the "broad road" without raising a finger to lead him back to the strait and narrow way from which she feared he might be straying?

She had been reading of late a good deal about the old days of chivalry, when knights were sent forth by their ladyes to fight the good fight, to protect the weak, to put down the wrong, and to keep themselves unspotted and pure. John had a vein of romance in his composition, as most boys have who have not had it all rubbed off by **too** much contact with this work-a-day world, and perhaps by appealing to all that was chivalrous in his nature she might make some impression for good upon him.

This evening he had been talking to her more confidentially than usual, and she seemed to know his true self, failings as well as noble qualities, better than she had ever done before. Something told her that this might be the turning-point in his life; his character seemed to be in that malleable state when any impression for good or evil might have its influence on his future. Should she, then, let the occasion go by unimproved, when his aspirations might be directed to higher objects than those which had hitherto engrossed him?

"John, I've been reading lately about some of the knights of old who were sent out in quest of adventures."

"Oh! do tell me about them," he said. "I always liked that style of thing, but it is no end of a bother to read about it."

She told him some of the best legends and tales, dwelling principally on those who had succeeded in keeping themselves *sans peur et sans reproche.*

"Now, I like that," said John reflectively, after she had finished. "I wish to goodness I had lived in those old times instead of these stupid ones! Wouldn't I have been your knight, Fanny, and you should have sent me on all sorts of perilous undertakings."

"Suppose I send you on one now, then," said Fanny, smiling.

"What do you want, your beef-essence or cod-liver oil? I'll get them, after your telling me all those splendid stories.' And John rose eagerly and with all the *empressement* of a knight ready for service.

Fanny smiled, but in a fluttering kind of a way, as if she were almost afraid to say what she really did want.

"Out with it! I'm your knight now, so you must buckle on my armor and send me off, even if it's for the unattainable roc's egg."

"I do long to buckle on your armor, but it is in a better service than mine can ever be. O John! will you let me send you forth to fight the good fight of faith?"

" Whew ! " replied her cousin, while h's countenance fell. " There's no fun in that. If you would tell me something real that I could do, like fighting a lion or bringing you the title-papers to your lost estate, or anything tangible."

" There will be plenty of lions for you to fight if you embrace this service ; and there is something really tangible you could do for me. and it is about a paper too. Oh ! it would make me so happy.'

" What is it ? " asked John eagerly, while he thought, " Now this is some- thing like."

" You won't be offended, will you? "

" Of course not ; do tell me."

" If you only knew how happy it

would make me if you were to sign the pledge!" And Fanny looked at him so entreatingly that he had to turn away and walk over to the window before he could answer.

"Anything but that, Fanny. Oh! why didn't you tell me to scale Pike's Peak or to bring you a feather from the Sandwich Islands?"

"O John! this is so much easier, and would· be of so much more real use to yourself."

"Now, **really**, Fanny," he replied, coming over to her sofa once more, "it is very unnecessary, your bothering your head about me. I've never been drunk in my life, at least not quite drunk, and there is not the slightest danger of such a thing."

" Not quite? Then you have been nearly! Oh! why didn't I ask you sooner, before temptation had commenced?" And Fanny clasped her hands in a despairing way, which made kind-hearted John very sorry, but made him feel more like going out of the room than giving any rash promise.

"You see I didn't want to bind myself,' he said, trying to speak consolingly. "It would be pretty hard on a fellow, if he could not take a social glass now and then, and I can assure you there is not the slightest danger of my going too far."

"Others more experienced than you say that the only safety is in total abstinence," said Fanny earnestly.

"Total abstinence be hanged! I did not mean that, Fan," he added more gently, "but it is so provoking, the way you women talk about what you don't know anything about." And feeling that this was his last and strongest argument, he hurried from the room, lest his cousin's pathetic answer might move him from his position.

Fanny sobbed bitterly, and for a time a sort of despair seemed to come over her. This was the end of all her bright visions of doing good: to be told that she did not know anything

about it!—that which had cast a cloud
over her early years, and whose effects
would ever remain in the chastened
sadness of a disposition naturally bright
and cheerful. No, there was no use in
trying, she thought, for a while; John
could just go his own way, and he
could not say that she had not, at least,
tried to prevent his downward course.
But after a while gentler and more hopeful thoughts came into her heart. God
had promised to hear the prayers of his
children, and are not these said to avail
much when offered up for another?
John was still so young that prayers
for him could not be hopeless, and could
she not ask Jesus to keep temptation

out of his way, so that, even if he did
not sign the pledge, he might be kept
from yielding to the power of drink?

Then she asked for help in subduing
her own impetuous disposition, so that
she might not drive him from the good
in her very efforts to draw him toward
it. She determined not to say any more
about it to him at present, but to pray
for him earnestly and faithfully night
and day.

She had no means of telling whether her
words might have had any effect. Although Mrs. Lodor was by no means an
advocate of total abstinence, it was not
her custom to have wine on the table
at meal-times, and Fanny never hap-

pened to be present when the wine-cup was handed around. All remembered too well the effect of that other glass, and so the subject was rather a tabooed one in her presence.

John also rather avoided her after that conversation; he had a sort of dread of yielding to those entreating brown eyes, and so for a while never remained in the room with her unless there were others present.

Fanny was much stronger now, and would fain have been allowed to resume her studies, but Dr. Palgrave told her honestly that it might shorten her life considerably. Once she might have thought this rather an additional reason for going back to school; for then life had seemed like a vacuum which she would readily have had lessened in any way; but her new-found treasure, her one pearl of great price, seemed to have lent additional value to life as so much consecrated to her Master's service. She longed to do something for him before his messenger should come, and it was with heart-felt thankfulness that she found she was not to be cut off entirely from the usefulness she so lovingly desired.

She had long felt like taking a class in the Sunday-school connected with the church of which she had become a member; and now that she had gained sufficient strength to warrant it, she eagerly sought the doctor's sanction, knowing that her aunt would not permit such an undertaking without it.

The doctor looked once again at her pale cheeks, felt her pulse, and listened to her breathing; but one glance at those earnest eyes weighed down all the testimony of these. He saw that some object of interest she must have, or it might even be worse for her than over-exertion; so that her heart was gladdened by a well considered "Yes."

And the wisdom of his decision was proved by its results. Fanny had now some definite object in life, and she tried to be conscientious in keeping her promise of not carrying her exertions too far.

She had just what she wanted—a class of boys from ten to thirteen years of age. They belonged to the poorer class of people, but some of them were bright and intelligent, and she enjoyed teaching them very much. After a while she began to visit their parents, Mrs. Lambert kindly going with her at first, and there was a good deal she could do for them in the way of advice and assistance; for not for naught had Fanny passed through that ordeal of her girlhood, and it was no wonder that many an old woman marvelled at the words of wisdom which came from her young lips.

It was natural that her greatest efforts should have been in the cause of temperance; and soon she found to her delight that every boy in her class was catching some of her enthusiasm. Willingly would each one there have signed the pledge, but she contented herself for the present with a promise of total abstinence, reserving the solemn vow which her paper contained for their riper years, when they could better understand it, as well as standing more in need of it. Soon they were vying with each other as to whose sixteenth birthday would come first; for this was the epoch at which she had promised to be their witness to this most solemn pledge.

And here we would say that this is
the surest way of spreading the cause
of temperance.   Enlist the young, get
hold of their sympathies, their principles,
their enthusiasm, engage these on the
good side before temptation has had a
chance to draw them over to the other.
Once they have yielded to that, the
very smell of liquor is enough to upset
them; but if they are firmly established
in the right, and have made up their
minds to stick to that, before they have
had a chance to enter upon the dangerous path called "moderate drinking,"
who can say that they are not safer than
those who trust to their own strength
to keep them from going too far?

CHAPTER V.

JOHN IS ENLISTED.

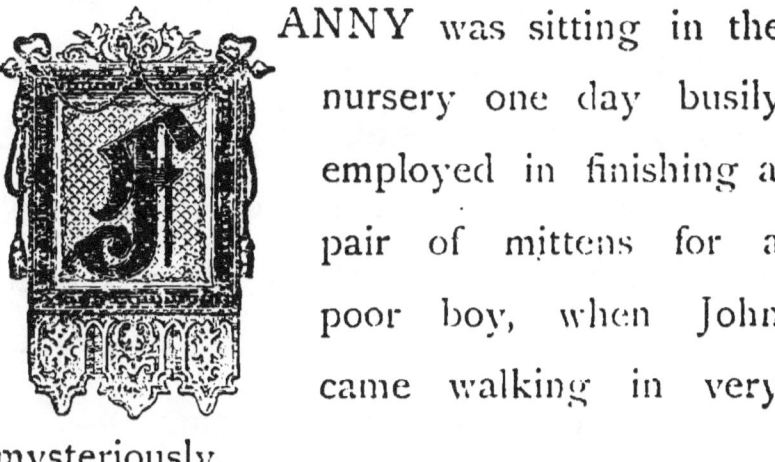ANNY was sitting in the nursery one day busily employed in finishing a pair of mittens for a poor boy, when John came walking in very mysteriously.

"I say, Fan, where's your pledge? I'll do anything for you now, to keep me from being what I saw last night."

Fanny looked up half alarmed, and, noticing her cousin's pale looks and blood-shot eyes, hardly dared ask the question which trembled on her lips.

" Have you been—? "

" No, not I; and, O Fanny! I've seen enough to make me shudder at it. Just to think of seeing him picked up out of a gutter!" And he pointed down toward his father's room.

Fanny held her breath in intense interest; the subject of her uncle's intemperance had never been broached before her, and it seemed a terrible thing even to be whispered about.

" Of course I knew that he drank a good deal of wine at his club, but he has always before been brought home in a genteel kind of way, in a carriage, and helped up-stairs by his driver, and no one is ever the wiser."

"How did it happen?" said Fanny, seeing that it would be a relief to John to tell her about it.

"Well, I believe they got into some kind of a row at his club last night, and the gov—father either left in a huff before the carriage came around, or else he said something that riled the others, and they turned him out. At any rate, the first thing I knew I was coming home with Harry Smith, and I heard a kind of row with a policeman. I wasn't quite myself at first, but as soon as I heard his voice I came to myself; and then, just think of it—Fanny having to help my own father out of the gutter!"

John laid his head on the table and indulged in such tears as he need not have been ashamed of. His cousin consoled him as best she might, and she saw that it would not be needful for her to "point the moral," but waited with a half-joyful thrill until John should again propose to sign the pledge.

As is so often the case, a great weight seemed lifted from his heart after he had communicated his trouble to another and had his cry out, and then it rather jarred on Fanny to hear him laughing at himself.

" I'm a sorry-looking knight, don't you

think so, Fan?" And he wiped his eyes and tried to fan away the last trace of tears; then, seeing that earnest look which he had once been so loath to satisfy, he said:

"Oh! you won't have to coax me. It's the only thing you ever asked your knight to do, and I resolved last night that I would lose no time. Where's your paper, and where the pen and ink?"

Fanny soon produced the articles, and her heart gave a thrill of ecstatic joy as she saw him sign his name to two papers, one of which he was to keep, and the other would remain with her as witness

"In the presence of Almighty God

and these witnesses, I do solemnly af-
firm that I will abstain from the use
of, or giving to others, as a beverage,
all spirituous and malt liquors, wine or
cider, for the space of my life.

Witnesses   JOHN LODOR, JR.

FRANCES PERCY.

—— ——."

John declared his intention of having
Harry Smith for his other witness, as he
was determined to clinch the resolution
which he had made in his presence the
night before.

Then the pledge was sealed in a
sweet way peculiar to cousins, and both
felt happier than they had done for
many a long day.

Fanny felt that her prayers were being answered in an unexpected manner, and she could go on in the work more hopefully now, seeing that John's own efforts were enlisted. He was very much touched when he found that she had been praying for him all these months; so much so that he promised to try and think about such things himself, and even to go to church, if he did not find it too stupid.

"You know I'll have to learn how to pray for father," he said, a little shyly.

"O John! suppose we make an agreement to do so at a certain hour every day, no matter where we may be—

if it is only a few words, sent up from the very heart."

"Do you really think it would do any good?" he asked doubtfully.

"Of course I do; if not in one way, then in some other. It always seems to me that the promise is greater to answer prayer, if two or more agree upon any one thing."

"Well, we can try. It won't do any harm, and won't take much time; for you know I am not used to this sort of thing, and could not stick at it very long at once."

"Oh! that does not make any difference," answered Fanny, eagerly; "you know we are told not to use vain repetitions, and I know, I feel, that if you unite with me in this that we shall be answered."

"Very well, then, twelve o'clock noon, I'll try and never forget; and don't you forget about me, for you know I haven't tried this thing of not taking even a glass of cider. It will come pretty hard at first, and I don't believe I can get along without your prayers for a while."

It was hardly necessary for Fanny to assure her cousin of her faithful continuance in this direction; she felt that she could do it with much better heart now, as success was at last beginning to crown her efforts.

She could hardly help hoping, too,

that the sense of shame from which her uncle must be suffering would have a beneficial effect upon him as well. She had not seem him that day, Mrs. Lodor having given out that he was sick in bed with a very bad headache. How Fanny wished and prayed that some holy influence might touch his heart, so that he might realize the error of his ways, and turn therefrom! She resolved to be doubly kind and attentive to him when he made his appearance, so that, if there ever chanced to be a fitting opportunity to plead with him, it might not be lessened by the thought of past neglect.

Fanny had now an acknowledged place

in her uncle's household; her quiet, gentle influence had not been without some effect on the ways of the family. Instinctively an almost reverential respect was shown for her by those who were affected, even unconsciously, by her unostentatious example.

Had she been a rival belle, Matilda and Clara no doubt would have disliked her in due proportion to her charms; but as it was, her aims in life seemed to have taken such an entirely different direction from theirs that their plans were rather furthered than interfered with by her presence in the house, as they found her always ready and willing to assist them. In their hearts they could not help respecting her, and, without knowing it, gave her opinions full weight in any discussion in which they might be engaged; .thus it was that Fanny sometimes had the casting vote when there was a difference of opinion between the two.

And now an important event was approaching which stirred the whole household into commotion. Matilda was to be married, and all sorts of gayeties were in prospect. Fanny had been able to keep free from such things, under the plea of respect to her father's memory; but two years had now elapsed since his death, and Matilda declared she would be very much hurt if Fanny would not consent to be her second bridemaid. Even Clara added her solicitations; it would not do to keep Fanny in the background any longer, she thought. It would be very convenient to have her to go out with sometimes after Matilda had gone; and, besides, the poor child had moped long

Now, Mrs. thought with a condescend- wish, man she remembered her own so wine at youth.

Fanny was considering the matter, and trying to decide on whatever might be right for her to do, when a discussion arose one evening whose issue she determined to make the test of her compliance with her cousin's wishes.

"What do you think, girls?" said Matilda, coming up into the nursery one evening after Mr. Calton's departure, and finding mother, sister, and cousin stitching away, as usual, at some of the finely-embroidered appurtenances of her trousseau.

"Well?" asked Clara curiously. ' You look as if you had b?ea tne whole You haven't broken it off, Matilda was Well, this would just fit me, ayeties did." 'ᵒ

"You selfish thing! But you needn't think it's come to that; but Stephen asked me as a great favor that we should not have any wine at our re- ception. Just think of it!"

"Oh! I am so glad," Fanny could not help saying.

"Now, that is two against me. I never heard of such absurd opinions; after a while people will be wanting to banish wine altogether. But, mother, do you think we ought to give way to it?"

Now, Mrs. Ledor had had reason to wish, many and many a time, that wine might have been banished altogether; but her pride on the subject was so great that she would not have had it known, by expressing her real opinions, how much she had suffered on this subject. Strange to say, she had never alluded in any one's presence to the subject of her husband's weakness (sin should be the true name for it), and now she shrank from entering into a discussion which might betray her, even to her own children.

"You and Mr. Calton must settle your own differences, Matilda; of course your father and I will pay for anything that you may order."

"There, that is always the way! If some one would only settle it for me! I hate not to do what Stephen requested so particularly, and yet it is so perfectly ridiculous."

"I wish you would let me decide it," said Fanny impetuously. "If you only knew, Matilda, the fearful responsibility of giving the first glass, or indeed any glass, to the young people who will be there. Oh! would you like to feel that you had been the tempter? Just think of it." And Fanny grew first crimson and then deadly pale in her excitement.

"That's all very well to talk about, but just remember how ridiculous it would seem to the hundreds of people who are used to taking it every day without being affected in the least."

"I doubt that very much," replied Fanny; "but even if it were so, ought they not to be willing to make some little sacrifice for the sake of those who might be led into sin by their example?"

"You do take such a serious view of everything, and then you imagine so much of what may never happen."

"It is happening every day in life, and it is every woman's duty to do all she can to prevent it. O Matilda! won't you decide on the right side?"

"Will you be my bridemaid if I do?"

"Oh! yes, anything," said Fanny joyfully.

"Well, I'll ask John's opinion before I make up my mind finally," said Matilda, who, as we perceive, was not a very decided character, but needed props and stays to uphold her, especially in any action liable to provoke the sneers of her chosen friends—"the world."

Fanny had no doubt how the matter would be settled if it depended on John's vote, and it would be a good opportunity, she thought, for him to avow the stand which he had decided to take in the cause of temperance. It was a pretty tough battle which he was fighting now, but hitherto he had come forth victorious from every trial, and, of course, with renewed strength for the next time.

He had not been what is called a "hard drinker," but had been fond of the exhilarating effects of a "social glass"; well for him that he had been brought up short in a career which, if unimpeded, would probably have brought him to the drunkard's grave.

His sisters were astonished when he announced his decision, and Matilda could not carry out what would have been her own wish in face of the opposition of lover, cousin, and brother.

And so the wedding passed off and was spoken of as a "strictly temperance affair"; by some with comments of approval, and by others with expressions of curiosity, knowing as they did that it was not in accordance with the general customs of the house. But the good leaven was doing its work, and Fanny could not but hope that in time its influence would reach even the master of the house.

CHAPTER VI.

FIRST BATTLE.

HILE John's resolutions were fresh in his mind it was comparatively easy for him to resist temptation; but gradually the effect of that terrible scene began to wear off, and then he almost wished that he had not been so hasty in signing the pledge.

"If I only had not bound myself!" he would think. "It seems like signing away my freedom." But that little slip of paper which his cousin had bound in blue as an emblem of truth still lay in the pocket "next his heart," as he had romantically told her he should always keep it, in the first enthusiasm of his good intentions. A safeguard it had been thus far; for whenever he had been invited by any of his young companions to take a social glass, he seemed to hear the rustle of the paper, or to see in his mind's eye his name signed to the solemn vow contained therein.

Harry Smith had indignantly refused to be the other witness, and had tried hard to ridicule John out of the idea of keeping his promise. Then, when he saw how useless was his attempt, he pretended to think that, if the pledge were destroyed, the promise would be also.

John guarded it most sacredly for a while—it seemed like the sign and seal of his young knighthood; but as his friend's influence began to resume its old sway over him, he could not but feel the strength of his good resolution gradually ebbing· away. How little do young people think how their whole future destinies may be influenced by their choice of companions; how hard it is to be good when in intimate companionship with those whose sympathies are in an entirely different direction ; and above all, how almost impossible it is to remain firm in a resolution when that resolution is daily, hourly being sapped and undermined by the example, advice, and entreaties of one's most intimate friend! O boys and girls! how careful should you be, in selecting your friends, to choose those who will help to lift you upward in the path of right. O fathers and mothers! how solicitous should you be to see your children choosing the right kind of associates at the time when their characters are most easily influenced for good or for evil.

Harry Smith had been encouraged by Mrs. Lodor in his intimacy with her son, because his parents were supposed to move in the "best society," but no pains had been taken to discover what his influence might be on John; the qualities of sobriety, industry, and a high aim in life were as nothing compared with style, wealth, and easy bearing.

Fanny had felt the change in the moral atmosphere, and had suffered from an almost indefinable dread that perhaps after all her efforts would prove in vain. How many a woman has felt sometimes that her prayers have been wasted, and all that mental agony of wrestling in which she has carried her heart's greatest wish to the throne of grace!. But the poet has told us to

> " Talk not of wasted affection :
> Affection never was wasted."

and the same may surely be said of prayer. Ofttimes we may not see the fulfilment of our wishes, and we may even be tempted to give up in despair; but we are told not to "be weary in well-doing, for in due season we shall reap if we faint not." Then go on, ye noble-hearted men and women who are using your efforts and prayers that Satan may be put down under our feet; and you who are praying with intense earnestness for some dear one who is straying from the fold, be not weary, for in due season you shall reap!

And this was what Fanny was doing, as she lay on the sofa in the nursery one day (for she had not been nearly so well of late), when John rushed in, in a state of great excitement, holding in his hand a torn and dirty piece of paper.

"O Fanny!" he exclaimed, "I have just escaped by the skin of my teeth. You can give up hopes of me; for I'm afraid I cannot hold out any longer."

"How was it, John?" And her eyes were dilated in a sort of horror, while she pressed her hand to her heart, which was fluttering nervously.

"Well, you see those fellows have been at me for ever so long about this thing, and to-day they managed to coax me into—never mind where, and they all got to drinking pretty hard, and the smell of it excited me, though, indeed, I don't care for it; and then they each tried to make me drink, but I seemed to feel this at my heart all the time, and somehow I could not break my word of honor when it was all written out in black and white. Well, Harry Smith knew this very well, and, with a hint from him, they were all teasing me about it, and I got excited, and there was a kind of joke as to whether they could get it away from me; it was understood that if they did, I would— but there, don't cry," as Fanny caressed the torn, rumpled paper, freshening it with her tears. "I didn't, you see."

"O John! I'm so thankful." And she looked as if he had been rescued from death. What mere death, indeed, could have been worse than that from which he had been rescued?

"The minute they all flew at me, trying to · get it, I seemed to realize all that it was to me; may be it was the 'contrairy' in me, but, at any rate, I determined they should not have it if I could help it, and so we had a pretty desperate struggle. I don't know which promise I ought to have kept, if they had managed to get it."

"You don't mean to say you promised them?"

"It was a kind of an implied promise, and I know they would have held me to it; but Mr.—never mind who—heard the row, and came in just in time. He didn't know what it was all about, or he would not have helped me; for of course it would have been to his interest if I had caved in. But here I am, safe and sound, and I do wish you could stop crying and talk to a fellow."

Fanny made a great effort to overcome her agitation, but she seemed stirred to the heart at the thought of her cousin's narrow escape; then it had been a blow to her to find that he could think any subsequent promise, or any accidental destroying of the mere sign of that promise, could in his eyes release him. She tried to express her thought to him as best she might, and he answered:

"I know that. Of course my promise to you can't be superseded by anything, even if both the papers were destroyed; but then a fellow can't keep his honor up to the very highest point when he's in such a set as that."

"I do wish you could get away from them all!" said Fanny fervently.

"I'll have to, if I want to be anything at all of a temperance man. Harry Smith is getting worse and worse every day. I wish you could get hold of him with your pledge."

"Why don't you try?"

"He just laughs at me; but I tell you

what, Fanny, it's you women that will have to do this work. I've had lots of pledges poked at me by other fellows, and it never entered into my head to sign one until you commenced preaching to me. Girls have no idea what they can do; and you don't know how many a young fellow has taken his first glass from the hands of a girl."

"Isn't it dreadful?" said Fanny, shuddering.

"Even some that are really trying to keep from it—that have promised their mother or sisters—go out to a party or on a New Year's call, and are ashamed to refuse, for fear of being laughed at and teased."

" If girls would only realize one-fourth the responsibility that rests on them!"

"If they all felt it like you do. I don't know where I would have been but for you. "

"It was not my persuasions so much as—"

"Yes, it was; for my first temptation on that awful night was to drown all thought of it by a good draught of wine, and then I seemed to remember about being your knight, and I thought may be that was one of the adventures by which I would be tested. So you see that romantic stuff did some good, though may be you did not think so at the time; and now I want you to see if you can fix that up for me again. You don't know what a help it is to feel my vow there every once in a while."

"O John! if I could only feel that it was engraved upon your heart, so that nothing could ever erase it."

"Well, I think it will be after a while, if you keep on remembering me in your prayers, and if I only could get away from those fellows for a while."

"Yes, that would be the best thing for you; couldn't you manage it some-how ?"

"I heard father talk about getting a travelling salesman for the firm, and he might as well try me as any one else; and then I could cut clear from Harry Smith, and make a new start when I come back in the fall."

"Oh! that would be just the thing. How soon would you start?"

"You're very anxious to get rid of a fellow; but you'll be going to the country soon anyhow, I suppose, and mind you get some more roses in your cheeks by the time I come back."

"I am going to try, for I would so love to be well and like other girls; but, John, in case—if God should be pleased not to make me well—"

"Now, don't talk that way, Fanny," said John, turning away hastily

"I don't want to be thinking about

myself, but in case anything does happen you will try and remember what we have talked about; it would be such a joy to me to think that I had had even the smallest influence in bringing one into the fold."

"Fanny, if I ever am brought into that fold—and I hope in time I may be—it will be your doings. I never used to think about such things at all until you came around, and the dear knows where I should have been now if it had not been for you; for I was getting awfully wild."

"Would you have room in your pocket for a little Testament? I could fasten this into it; and then you would read

some every day or evening, wouldn't
you?"

"To please you I would; and I don't
think it is so dull as I used to before
I had begun to feel the need of it.
And now I must go have a talk with
father."

It was soon settled that John could
attend to the business his father had
spoken of, and so for a while be removed from those whose companionship had
been so bad for him. Not that he could
go out of the reach of temptation—for,
wherever he might be, that would be
sure to assail him; but since that last
talk with his cousin his heart seemed to
be opening more and more to good in-

fluences; and when, before he bade her good-by, she gave him the little Testament containing his pledge, he felt as if he were indeed a knight starting out in search of high and noble adventures.

CHAPTER VII.

SAD YET HOPEFUL DAYS.

 OUR health, Miss Mabel." And young Mr. Eldredge raised the glass to his lips.

"Indeed, if you only would not!" And the young girl put out her hand entreatingly.

"Why! what's this new freak?"

"I've just begun," replied the other with some hesitation, "to doubt whether we have been doing right; indeed, I never used to think about it at all."

"And pray what put these 'doubts' into your head?"

"There is a young lady staying here —oh! she is so lovely—and we had an argument on the subject last night."

"Lovely young ladies condescend to argue sometimes, do they?"

"Where a principle is concerned, and where there is any chance of convincing, yes," replied Mabel firmly.

"I did not know there was ever any chance of convincing you, once you had made up your mind."

"But you see I had not made it up about this; for I had never thought much about it until Fanny—Miss Percy —got to talking."

"And now it is made up irrevocably, I suppose." And he set the brimming glass upon the table with a mock disconsolate air.

"Yes; I don't intend to take one drop myself, and shall do all I can to keep others from doing so."

"Heroic sacrifice!"

"No, it is not," answered the other candidly. "You know I don't care for it much myself, although I suppose I shall miss it a little at first; but the worst part will be the being laughed at. But I can bear even that rather than do what I would feel to be wrong."

"I really can't see the harm in it; of course everything has its limits, and

I would not give a snap for the man or woman who had not self-control enough to keep within bounds."

"That's what so many have said; but I wish you could hear her talk. You would believe then that better men than you have thought the same thing, and themselves gone too far."

"Thank you, but that is what I call begging the question; for if I can prove it to be true in my case, I certainly am not responsible for their weakness."

"But you have not proved it; for no man knows at what time his weakness may be overcome, and the only safety for all is in total abstinence."

"There is certainly no danger for such as you," replied he, noticing how she seemed to include herself in the assertion.

"Even if there were not—and I would not dare to say so—the example to others would be harmful; and what would such a sacrifice as that be compared to the pleasure of helping on a great and glorious cause?" And her eyes shone bright with her youthful enthusiasm as she spoke.

"Now, it is too warm to get excited; but let us go down the mountain-side and sit under those fine old forest-trees." And, with a gay laugh and joke, he tried to divert her from the thought which had gained such sway over her. Perhaps he did not wish to dwell on a discussion which, if it succeeded in convincing him, would involve such a sacrifice on his part; but she was not to be so easily diverted.

"There she is now!" she exclaimed eagerly as they reached the fine, wide veranda of the mountain-house at which they were spending their summer.

Fanny looked up from her book, and gave a sweet smile as her new friend drew near. She is much paler and thinner than when we saw her last, and there is a certain ethereal expression about her which speaks unmistakably of the land to which she is hastening.

Mabel introduced her friend, and almost immediately afterwards the subject
which was uppermost in her thoughts.
It was one of such painful interest to
Fanny that she was apt to become excited when discussing it; but no one
could help being impressed by her intense enthusiasm, than which nothing is
more contagious.

Mr. Eldredge, like Mabel, had never
before given the subject much serious
thought; he had always been taught
to consider it the correct thing to take
his glass of wine after dinner, but of
course had never more than once or
twice taken even a drop too much.
But now he began to think of his

responsibilities in respect to others, and perhaps, he thought, even his small influence might do something to retard or further the cause of temperance. At any rate, he would give the subject due consideration, and at least abstain from wine until he had made up his mind on one side or the other.

Mabel was not the only friend whom Fanny had made during her sojourn among the mountains. None who conversed with her could help being interested in the bright, intelligent girl who seemed to be hastening away so fast from the things of this world.

She was trying hard to resign herself to Him who alone holds the issues of life and death; and though, had the choice been with her, she might have asked to be allowed to serve him a little while longer, she knew that it would be all for the best if she were called away. Would there not be some service of love for her in that other fair, bright world?

Her relations were spending the summer at a more fashionable watering-place; but mountain air had been pronounced better for her, and her aunt had agreed to Mrs. Lambert's kind offer to remain with her during the vacation.

It is strange how one or two people of decided character can sometimes affect the whole tone of a house.

Not many weeks had elapsed after the arrival of these two before a marked change in one respect might have been observed. Fanny's influence over Mabel seemed to be the starting-point; for that young lady was not one to be ashamed of her colors.

Day after day the subject was eagerly discussed, almost every day adding at least one new convert to the good cause. Most of the guests were of those who had never before given the subject their serious consideration; but now that they had begun to do so, they could hardly fail to be convinced by the almost self-evident arguments which were used.

Mabel and Mrs. Lambert did most of the talking on the temperance side; for Fanny was too shy, as well as too weak, to discuss the subject with more than one or two at a time. But she was well content to supply the pledges, and to be witness for any number of signers; and there were some who, without binding themselves by promise, showed by their actions that they would act up to the conditions of the vow.

A glad thrill passed over Fanny as, when she was parting with Mabel, the latter whispered:

" I am so glad I have met you; you don't know how much good you have done me."

How thankful Fanny felt that God had allowed her, weak and useless as she had once felt herself to be, to do something in his service!

And now there remained one more work for her; if she only might be permitted to see that accomplished, how willingly, how gladly would she go! Her uncle—could she leave him without one effort to save him from the abyss to which he was hastening?—for her sad experience told her that the habit was growing stronger and stronger, and perhaps before long it would be too late to attempt to break it, even if he should be willing to bring all his strength and energy to the task. But as yet hope whispered

to her that it was not too late, and
perhaps he would listen to an appeal
from her. These thoughts occupied her
on the journey home, and she determined to make the effort on the first opportunity after her arrival. Judge, then,
of her disappointments when, on coming
home, she found no one there to welcome her but Mrs. Lodor, her uncle
having decided to remain a few weeks
longer at the urgent solicitations of
Clara and Nettie.

If she had only spoken long ago!
But then something had always told her
that he would merely laugh at her.
Perhaps, after all, it would be better to
write—she could always speak more free-

ly with her pen than with her tongue; and so at intervals, as her strength would permit, she wrote a long letter to him, beseeching him, as he valued happiness in this world and salvation in the next, that he would break off from that habit which was growing stronger and stronger upon him. It was a truly eloquent appeal, coming as it did from the depths of her heart and being written in such a prayerful, earnest spirit. But perhaps even it might have had a less powerful effect had it been received under different circumstances. For before the letter was sealed a sudden change for the worse came over Fanny. Mrs. Lodor telegraphed for her husband, but the message travelled around from cne place to another in search of him, and by the time he had received it, and was hurrying home, the last message had come for her whose spirit was now winging its flight to another world.

It was a great shock to the whole family; for none of them, except Mrs. Lodor, had realized that the seal of death was on her brow, and even she had never dreamed, until the last few days, that she would go so soon.

John was sent for, and arrived just in time to see his dear cousin laid in her last resting-place. His spirit was overwhelmed within him as he remained at the grave long after the others had gone, trying to reconcile himself to the absence of her who had been, as it were, the guiding-star of his life.

He had succeeded in retaining self-command as long as the others were near, but as soon as the last carriage had driven away he gave way unrestrainedly to " that sound of all sounds the most painful to hear—the sobs of a man."

At first it was a rebellious as well as an overwhelming agony, but after a while something of her spirit seemed to subdue him; and then, remembering the little Testament which he always carried faithfully about him, he took it out, and read such portions over and over

again as he found most comforting
to his soul.

It was a good, a softened time for
such thoughts to take possession of his
heart, and soon he sent up such an
earnest prayer for help and strength
as he never remembered offering before.
He resolved to amend his life with the
help of Him who is ever ready to help
a soul on in the path of right, and
to consecrate himself, as far as he was
able, to his service.

Then he rose up, and, gathering a
little flower which was growing near,
pressed it in his book as a memento
of that hour, and of her who had exercised such an influence for good over him.

When he reached home it was after dark, and he would fain have gone to his own room to "commune with his own heart and be still"; but his father called him into the library and handed him a letter which he had evidently just read, and which had affected him almost beyond control. It was Fanny's letter, the last she had ever written; and coming, as it did, like a voice from the dead, it had stirred all the best, the noblest feelings in Mr. Lodor's nature.

"Read it, John; your mother found it among her papers. It is just like her—so sweet, so earnest."

John complied with his father's request with tender yet painful thrills of feeling. It did seem as if she spoke to them; and yet, how long would it be before they would hear that dear voice again?

John broke down before he had half finished, and then, throwing his arms around his father's neck, exclaimed:

"Father, you will think of what she says, won't you?"

"I intend to try, my dear boy, and, God helping me, will be a different man from this time."

Then John told him of some of his own temptations, and how he had succeeded in abstaining for more than a year past. The father felt encouraged by his son's sympathy, and the fact that each was struggling in the same path gave them a feeling of companionship which would make the future easier for both.

John, new to the work as he was, tried to lead his father to the highest Source of strength, sure that this would be the only true safeguard. Did any one ever succeed in reforming his life who went to the work trusting entirely in his own strength?

CHAPTER VIII.

WHAT SHOULD NOT HAVE HAPPENED.

T was no easy work which those two had before them. Habit had so wound itself about Mr. Lodor's very being that every day brought with it its own temptation. John had taken it as a kind of sacred legacy from his cousin to watch over his father and keep temptation from him as much as possible. The latter voluntarily gave him a solemn promise that he would try with

all his strength of will to resist temptation. Wine was banished from the
house, and Mr. Lodor withdrew from
his club, which had been the principal
scene of temptation for him. There were
other places which he could not so well
avoid, where the wine-cup was apt to
be presented to him; but there was
John, always ready to hand, a faithful
watcher over his father's well-being.

For a while all other objects in life
seemed to bend to this, and perhaps
the very sacrifices which the task involved served to deepen the impression
for good which had been made upon
him, and to mould his character after a
higher form than would once have seemed

possible. Fortunately, there were those who were ready to help him in the new life which he had chosen. The minister of Fanny's church had become, through her, interested in the different members of her uncle's family, and it was to him that John now went for advice and guidance at a time when he so much needed it.

Mr. Hervey received him with open arms, listening with interest to his account of his past life, and of the great desire he had to devote the rest of it to his Saviour, and especially to be an active worker in the great cause of temperance. He knew that, could Fanny look down upon him and see him engaged in this work, it would give her more joy than to have seen him heaped up with worldly honors and riches; but even if there were no possibility of her knowing, he himself could feel that he was fulfilling her desires, and that he was still, as it were, bound on the errands of knighthood in which she had engaged him. And now he was going into the highest service of all; for the great Master was captain of the army in which he hoped soon to be enlisted as a regular soldier, and on his strength would he rely to deliver him from temptation.

Fanny had left a message for him, that she should like him to take her class in Sunday-school, and it seemed like a fitting beginning of his Master's work. As we have said, the boys were mostly from the poorer classes, and generally ignorant, and John felt much more at ease with such scholars than he would have done with those in his own sphere. It seemed more, too, like accomplishing something to work with those who had but few home advantages. Most of them were already enlisted in the temperance cause, and those who had not signed the pledge were looking forward to doing so on their sixteenth birthday. Fanny had left some forms to be given out as each eventful day came around, and there were but few of those boys who did not treasure his up as a sacred relic for years afterward.

John soon found his way into their various homes, and it often made him heart-sick to find how wide-spread was the evil of intemperance. Sometimes he felt tempted to give up in despair; for what could he do against such a mighty foe? Was it not like trying to beat down the waves? But then he would remember that others were engaged in the same work, and that, even if only a few were saved, it would be worth all the prayers, all the labors, all the anxiety that had been expended upon them. But there was One above who could render fruitful their labors;

and who shall despair while God is on
our side?

And so the first year passed away,
sometimes fraught with hope and at others full of discouragement; but he work-
ed on through all, and at the end of the
year could look back and see some fruits
which gladdened his heart.

His father, at least, had succeeded beyond his most sanguine hopes; it had
only been by a careful avoidance of
temptation, sometimes rushing away from
it in a manner that caused no little
surprise to the uninitiated.

One day the two had been parted
for a longer time than usual, John having been on a collecting expedition for

the firm, and Mr. Lodor going with his wife to call on young Mrs. Hervey; for their minister had lately been taking a bride unto himself.

John felt happier than he had done for a long time; the keen edge of his grief was wearing off, and he could now think of his cousin as of a sweet influence which had been lent to his life for a little while, and then taken where no pain could reach her, after her mission on earth had been accomplished. Yet the influence on his life would never cease, he hoped; time rather seemed to deepen than to erase the impression which had been made, and any one who could have seen that well-

read Testament would have easily be-
lieved that it was still his most sacred
treasure.

He had felt particularly happy lately
about his father and mother. At his
earnest request they had been going to
church with him, and it had seemed to
give a common bond of sympathy between the three. Perhaps after a while
they would join him altogether on the
road in which he was travelling; nothing could exceed the joy that such
an event would give him, and he sent
up an earnest prayer for its consum-
mation. The joyful light had not entirely faded from his face when, turning suddenly around a street-corner, he

met his mother, looking more worried and anxious than he had seen her for a long time. He greeted her affection-ately, and enquired for his father.

"I am just looking for him; he left Mr. Hervey's more than an hour ago. Oh! haven't you seen him?"

There was a tone of ill-concealed anguish in the question which startled John exceedingly.

"Which way did he go? Have you been looking for him long? Have you any idea where he is?"

"I am afraid, John, I am so afraid that—indeed, I don't know where he is; but he took something at Mrs. Hervey's, and I'm so afraid it brought the taste for more."

John uttered a hasty exclamation and hurried off, knowing now only too well where he would be likely to find his father. His heart was full of bitter indignation. Was all the work of a year to be destroyed by the thoughtless act of a woman who certainly ought to have known better?—the wife of a minister, and, if he was not mistaken, the daughter of one as well.

Long and mortifying was his search, and at last he found his father in a tavern which he had passed almost unnoticed more than once in his search. His heart ached as he tried in vain to rouse him; it had been so long since Mr. Lodor had taken any liquor that

what would once have had little effect
had now thrown him into a stupor.

His son sent for a carriage, and the
two were soon on that sad homeward
journey which John would never forget.

He leaned back in the carriage, trying to bring peace once more into his
troubled breast; but it had resigned its
dominion for the present, and in its stead
reigned wrath and indignation.

What should he do? Impulse would
have led him to write a most scathing letter to the one who had been the cause
of this fresh trouble; but delicacy and
courtesy forbade, for was she not the
wife of his friend, a minister of the holy
Gospel?

At first he felt that if he could not give vent to the indignant feelings which she had caused, he must try and hold his peace altogether; but further consideration told him that it was his duty to go to Mrs. Hervey and lay the case candidly before her; it would certainly have some effect in convincing her how very wrong had been her course of conduct, and perhaps prevent a like misfortune to others who would be likely to call upon her.

He chose the next morning for his visit, as not being one of her reception days; and of course he would prefer finding her alone. And not a moment was to be lost; for who could tell how many more might be tempted the next week by the same fair hands?

At first Mrs. Hervey excused herself; but John sent up a message that he had come on urgent business, and that he would try and not detain her a moment longer than was necessary.

After what seemed like two or three hours, the young bride made her appearance, dressed very handsomely in an elaborate morning dress; but she might as well have had on a calico, as far as John was concerned, for he was too intent on his errand to be dazzled by her appearance.

He had to summon all his gentlemanly instincts before he could respond at all pleasantly to her friendly greeting.

She was very much astonished indeed when he explained his errand, and expressed regret .at having "just happened" to offer wine to the wrong person.

"We have always been accustomed to it at home, and my father thought each one should be able to keep himself within bounds; so that, after all, no one can be blamed but the one who takes it."

"I'm sure Mr. Hervey does not think so, and I should not think you would either after what I have just told you."

"It is a pity, and I apologize to you for it. Alec did want to do without it altogether at our receptions, but it seemed so inhospitable to me that I could not agree with him, and so I had my own way about it."

"May I ask whether you intend to continue having it?" asked John, hardly able to restrain his wrath.

"Our receptions are over now, but, if I have my way, we will offer it to our friends for hospitality's sake; though I can assure you you need not worry about your father, for we will be more careful in future about him."

"It is perhaps too late for that; but, O Mrs. Hervey! if you would only think of the terrible responsibility you are incurring. You know not who else may be in equal danger; will you not place their highest well-being above the mere wish of appearing kind and sociable?"

"I really cannot take the same view of it that you do. There never was a better man than my father, and we always had it on the table at dinner; indeed the very wine we are using now was a present from him, or I don't believe my husband would have brought it."

"But cannot you see from what has just occurred that your views must be wrong ones?"

"Such a thing might not occur again in ten years; but I will promise to be more careful in future as to whom I offer it."

"The only really careful way is not

to give it to any one; you know not
which of your guests may have a latent taste for it, nor which may be
thrown back into bad habits by means
of one glass."

But the little lady was still uncon-
vinced, and John came away in despair,
resolving, at least, that that should be
his father's last visit while the present
state of affairs lasted.

Mr. Hervey was a strictly temperate
man himself, and had even preached
several sermons in mission chapels on the
subject of total abstinence; but these had
been mostly for the poorer classes, and
he had rather agreed with his wife in
thinking that among their own friends

there would be no harm in a social glass, depending on each to keep himself within proper bounds.

He heard of Mr. Lodor's misfortune from another source than either his wife or John, and it was with a very mortified feeling that he went around to see the latter.

John could not, in sincerity, greet him with his usual cordiality; for he felt that he had been in some measure to blame in so yielding to his wife's influence as to permit the wine to be offered to their guests. Of course he had not been present when Mr. Lodor had taken that fatal glass, or he would have interfered in his case, knowing the danger for him; but, in John's opinion, he should not have allowed any of it to be used as a beverage.

"How's your father this evening, John?"

"A little better, no thanks to Mrs. Hervey," replied John, trying to be gruff; he must have some way of relieving his pent-up feelings.

"Remember that you are speaking of my wife," replied the other with dignity.

"I do remember it, Mr. Hervey; but I cannot forget that it was she who offered him the glass that has thrown him back, perhaps, to where he was before."

"I hope not; but really, John, I had no idea of his coming without you, or I would have told Mrs. Hervey."

"I thought he was going to a perfectly safe place when he went to your house. O Mr. Hervey! if any place should be removed from temptation, it would seem that it would be the house of a minister of the Gospel; and I am afraid yours is not the only one where such is not the case."

"Yes, I acknowledge that it was wrong. Had I been more decided in my objections, Mrs. Hervey, no doubt, would have yielded to my wishes; but I never before have seemed to have the subject brought so close home as in this instance. I am very deeply sorry, my boy." And he extended his hand, as if asking for forgiveness. "I need not tell you that the wine shall be banished *in toto*, and I know I can succeed in convincing my wife of the reasonableness of this decision."

John felt his doubts on the latter point, but not any concerning the promise; and it was some consolation to feel that what had been such a severe trial might prove a lesson never to be forgotten by those who had been the cause of the misfortune.

For a time his father seemed plunged into a state almost of despair by this one recurrence of the old habit; but

John gradually reasoned him into a more hopeful state, knowing that the very worst thing would be for him to retain the idea that there was "no use of trying any more."

The former guardianship was renewed, and the faithful son could only go on hoping and praying that his father would one day learn to lean on the one only sure Safeguard, compared to which all human strength is nothing.

CHAPTER IX.

NETTIE.

OW often it happens to be easier to show one's colors among strangers than with the nearest and dearest! For more than a year John had been using most intense exertions in the great cause of temperance, and yet, strange to say, scarcely a word on the subject had been exchanged with his sisters Clara and Nettie. The former was still a fashionable young lady, intent on the gayeties and pleasures of this life,

while the latter had just emerged from
the chrysalis school-girl state, on the *qui
vive* for enjoyment and fun. She was a .
sprightly, attractive girl, with more character than had fallen to the lot of either
of her sisters, but as yet having no
higher aim in life than, as she expressed it, to have a good time.

How her character would develop,
whether the influence she was sure to
carry with her would or would not be
potent for good, depended in a great
measure on whether her boat would be
steered in the track of brother or sister
in starting out upon the great ocean of
life.

Had John only known how much depended on his influence, things might have gone differently for a while, and much sorrow would have been saved; but, to tell the truth, he did not feel very well acquainted with his sisters, and was rather shy about speaking of the subjects which lay nearest his heart.

Nettie was soon the centre of a circle of admiring friends, thoughtless girls and young men, most of whom were attracted by her vivacity and life. Clara might have felt a pang of jealousy sometimes, had it not been that her beauty had acquired for her a prestige which even her younger sister's attractions could not throw into the shade. The two girls went out constantly together, and were beginning to look forward to giving their first party for that winter. There had been no gayeties at Mrs. Lodor's since Fanny's death. Clara had diverted her mind from the " dulness," as she called it, by travelling and visiting among her friends, but now that Nettie was to " come out," and the house would be thrown open once more, she could bear to return to it.

She held her brother John's " notions," as she called them, in a sort of contempt, and was almost insensibly influencing Nettie to regard them in a like manner. The gay young people with whom they mingled were, as a general thing, neither religious nor perfectly temperate, and it was but natural that Nettie's views should receive some coloring from theirs; and yet sometimes an undefined feeling of dissatisfaction would come into her heart. She had a most lively and affectionate remembrance of her cousin Fanny; and even after having been, as she had thought, at the height of enjoyment among her young companions, the contrast between their conduct and views and those of her dear cousin would occasionally force itself upon her.

And yet she continued to allow herself to be influenced by those who her higher sense told her were neither elevating nor improving. Circumstances had thrown her among them, and she enjoyed their admiration too much to be willing to withdraw herself from it.

"I'll have a good time while I'm young, and settle down after a while, and think about the things Fanny used to talk about," she would say to herself, after having experienced one of those sudden raps at her heart which would every once in a while remind her that there was something else to live for than mere enjoyment.

She rather avoided her brother John, lest he might "preach to her"; and there was a dim sense that she could not hold out against such preaching, and especially if he brought Cousin Fanny's name in to give weight to his arguments. This was particularly the case in regard to the question of total abstinence. Nettie liked an occasional glass of wine; it exhilarated her so, and made her more lively and witty than usual. She did not want to realize that she was treading on dangerous ground in thus using it as a stimulus, nor did she wish to feel that it was wrong to offer a glass now and then to her young friends. Not that she had an opportunity of doing so at home—for, as we have said, wine had long ago been banished from Mr. Lodor's—but she often assisted her young lady friends in administering the rites of hospitality, and then it was that her fair hand would become the hand of the tempter. For, with few exceptions, wine was considered a *sine quâ non* in most of the houses where she visited, and she took rather a delight in showing that it was not her fault that she could not offer it in her own home.

It was the only drawback to her enjoyment of the "delightful" party which she and Clara gave that winter.

"It seemed so mean not to have it," she said to the latter, "after receiving it so liberally everywhere else. No wonder Fred Warrington and Harry Smith had gone away early."

For Harry Smith, John's quondam friend, had drifted back into the old path which led to Mr. Lodor's hospitable mansion; not now, as in days of yore, to visit John—for, like Nettie, he rather avoided the sermon which would (he thought) have been sure to follow an interview with him—but a far brighter attraction in his eyes was luring him on. O Nettie, Nettie! would that your influence might have been used to lift him up to higher paths than any he had yet chosen.

For Harry was in that softened state when "one woman's" word may go so far. Oh! why was that word not spoken which might have turned him back ere it was too late?

He really was making an effort to be a decent and respectable member of society—was struggling manfully against his besetting sin; for he knew there would be no hope for him if that were not conquered.

But he was struggling all alone, and his will was weak to resist, especially when certain bright eyes looked at him so coaxingly, begging him to drink "only one glass" for her sake.

John knew nothing of all this; for he seldom went into the gay company in which his sisters mingled, and at home there was no chance of his seeing, what was now no infrequent occurrence, Harry Smith drinking the health of his sister Nettie. He knew that he was one of the many who frequented their house, and was glad to see him more steady and settled-looking than of yore, attributing the change in part to his being intimate at such a strictly temperate house as their own. Could Nettie only have . received one word of warning! Could she only have known what lay in her power for good or for evil, would not the scales have turned differently?

Oh! let me entreat the young girls who may happen to read this book to let their influence be brought to bear on the side of the good and the right. How do you know any more than Nettie did to whom you may be offering the tempting cup? How do you know but that your example in taking now and

then the social glass may be the means
of causing some of the weaker brethren
to fall? Pause and think ere it be too
late! Would it not be better to sacrifice
some little pleasure of your own, even if
you think there is no possible danger for
you, than to incur the remotest possibility of causing another to sin?

Harry felt within himself that the only
safety for him would be in total abstinence; and though he was too proud to
accede to the solicitations that he would
sign the pledge, he gave his word of
honor that he would abstain positively
for six months.

It was John Lodor who extracted this
promise from him at last; for he began

to feel that there were more than the usual reasons for his wishing to see Harry a strictly temperate man. It was a vague, undefined fear which had entered into his heart, and as yet he had spoken to no one on the subject; a strange reserve seemed to be deepening between him and Nettie, and his natural delicacy forbade his saying anything which might wound her maidenly feelings. Perhaps, after all, his fears might be groundless, or it might be that anything said in disparagement of Harry would have the very effect of warming her in his defence. No; he could not bring himself to speak to her, but would use his utmost endeavors to save Harry, and then leave the issue in higher hands.

His heart bounded high with hope of helping another fellow-creature into the right path when Harry, not unwillingly, gave him that promise. Little did he think that his own sister would be the first one to cause that promise to be broken, and little did Nettie think what she was doing when she placed that glass of wine to his lips.

Do not blame her too much, you who only drink it occasionally, and then only when no one is by who may be injured by your example. You know not who may be injured by it; the little brother sitting at your side, apparently unobservant, but whose keen eyes nothing escapes; the servant who waits on you respectfully, and who eagerly drains the few remaining drops from the glass as soon as your back is turned—these, and others who may be far enough from your thoughts, but not out of the circle of your influence—these may, at some future time, rise up and point to you as the one whose example led them into the first temptation.

CHAPTER X.

ONLY ONE GLASS.

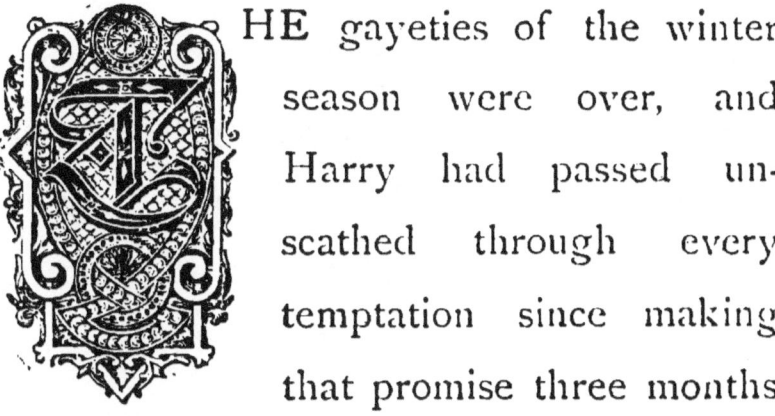 HE gayeties of the winter season were over, and Harry had passed un-scathed through every temptation since making that promise three months ago. And this he had managed without even letting Nettie know that he was under such a promise; for he had avoided having to refuse wine at her hands, dreading her persuasions or laughing surprise.

Summer was now approaching, and a delightful picnic was in contemplation in honor of Nettie's birthday on the thirteenth of June. It was to be a very select affair, being limited to twenty intimate friends. The father of one of these had had prepared for the purpose grounds attached to his lovely country-seat about five miles from the city, and of easy access either by steam or passenger railway.

It was a delightful change after the hot, dusty city to find themselves, after a half-hour's ride, in those cool, shady woods, looking up through their leafy branches to the soft blue sky beyond.

Everything seemed conspiring together

for their happiness—a soft, balmy air breathed through the forest, the sweet birds sang around them, and the best of spirits seemed to pervade the whole company.

The dinner is generally the all-important event at a picnic, and nothing could have been more tempting than the one these young people had brought with them to-day.

A long table had been erected a few days before, and this they now covered with their snowy-white table-cloths, which gave it a more home-like appearance than is often the case at picnics.

Great fun they had in setting the table, and many a laugh was excited at the awkwardness of the young gentlemen, who probably professed more ignorance of domestic affairs than the occasion demanded.

Merrily the joke went round as they seated themselves, each one quite accidentally, as it were, finding himself next to the very one whom he would have chosen for a companion.

Nettie laughed and talked with Harry, promising him something very good for dessert if he was a good boy and obeyed all her behests.

"You know I always do that, Miss Nettie," he replied in the same jesting way; but his cheek grew a little pale when the promised reward was produced and proved to be a bottle of very fine wine.

The other young gentlemen needed no persuasion to drink the health of the very lovely young lady whose birthday they were celebrating ; but Harry held back for some little while, remembering his promise, and remembering, too, what one violation of that promise might lead to. Oh! why did he not jump up with determination and flee from temptation, as would have been his only safe mode of escape? But he lingered—refusing, to be sure, but not with the same firmness as at first; for would not Nettie be hurt at his apparent want of cordiality in cele-brating her birthday?

"There! only a few drops, even if you don't take the whole glassful." And she actually held it up to his lips, even tipping the glass, so that the liquor would either have to go into his mouth or fall down on his immaculate shirt-bosom.

"Well, one might as well be killed for a sheep as for a lamb," said Harry, trying to laugh, while he drained the glass, and then held it out for more.

Nettie felt a little frightened at what she had done, and shook her head, saying:

"One glass is the limit, you know; and, besides, it's all gone now, you took so long to make up your mind."

"You never were so stingy before,

Nettie; but I know what I am in for now. Come, boys, let's take a swim while the girls clear the table; we'd be sure to smash all their dishes if we tried to help them."

Some of them agreed to go, regardless of the cautions of the more prudent ones, who considered it too early in the season, and knew, besides, that it was not good to bathe just after a hearty meal.

The adventurous ones went off in search of the creek, however, leaving the others to entertain themselves as best they might after the dishes had been repacked in the baskets.

The afternoon was not so pleasant as

the forenoon had been; dark, gusty
clouds were gathering, and now and
then the low, distant roll of thunder
might have been heard. The others
were too much preoccupied with their
sports and flirtations to take any heed
of the approaching storm, but Nettie's
heart seemed oppressed with a corre-
sponding darkness, and every fresh in-
dication of the storm . brought with it
renewed anxiety.

At last the drops began to patter,
and the others were aroused to a
sense of the situation. Such a hurry
and scurry as there was for baskets,
umbrellas, and water-proofs ! and then
they rushed off pell-mell to the railroad

station, about a quarter of a mile distant. They were thoroughly drenched
by the time they reached it; but fortunately there was a train due in a very
few moments, so that it would not be
very long before home would be reached
and their clothing changed.

The train was just in sight when the
bathers made their appearance in the
distance, and it was a question whether
they would be able to reach it. Nearer
and nearer came the train, while the
young gentlemen ran hurrahing, hoping
to induce the conductor to wait for them
if they were not quite on time.

Nettie felt herself jostled in, and would
fain have watched to see whether their

friends would reach them; but the others hurried on, passing through one car after another, trying to find seats for the party. At length Nettie was seated, and happened to look out of the window just in time to see Harry getting on, as the train was starting, a car or two behind them. She felt very much relieved, for she had had an indefinable dread that something had happened to him; but now all must be right, and he would soon make his way to her.

But the moments rolled by, and he did not come. No doubt he was repaying all her anxiety by indulging in a cigar; for it was the smoking-car, she thought, which he had entered. The journey

seemed much longer than in the morning; there were more detentions and con-
siderable backing, which almost made her
sick.

When they reached the city it seemed
strange that Harry did not hasten to her
and escort her home; but she certainly
would not wait for him after the way he
had acted, and so she hurried on with
the friends who were in the first car, and
did not see the blanched cheeks and
startled looks of those who were follow-
ing after.

CHAPTER XI.

A GREAT CHANGE.

H ! the horror of those en-
suing days. Oh! the an-
guish which nothing could
soothe; for it could not
long be kept from Nettie
the terrible fate which had
awaited Harry as he stepped on to that
car; how, not having the usual command
over himself, he had lurched to one side
as the car started, and, falling down between that and the next car, had been
picked up apparently lifeless when the

train had gone by. Oh! if she only had
not known that it was her fault, her
fault; for did it not come out gradually
that the young men, instead of going to
the creek, had made their way to a tavern which Harry had noticed on the
roadside in the morning, and which he
had felt he must reach, now that the
taste for liquor had been reawakened by
that one fatal glass? Here he would
have remained all night, perhaps, after
satiating himself, had not the others fairly pulled him away, with just sense
enough left for themselves to know that
they ought to be moving homewards.

Had they been entirely sober, Harry's
fate might have been different; but they

were far enough in advance of him to reach the car in front of the one he tried to enter, and they had taken it for granted that he had reached it safely, or rather they had not enough sober sense left to give the subject any thought.

And now his life hung on that one slender thread, which every day was expected to snap asunder. Nettie could not bear to think of it, and yet the thought haunted her day and night—that fatal glass; and it was her fault, and where would he be this time to-morrow? Oh! if it might only turn out to be a horrible dream; then indeed would she have received lesson enough, and never, never again would she handle the fearful cup which had proved so terrible! But no; the days rolled by, convincing her that it was no dream, but a terrible reality. At times it seemed as if reason might go from her, but her naturally strong constitution bore up under the shock it had received, and she was not even sick.

At first a stony kind of reserve seemed to settle down upon her, and, though she listened and watched eagerly for any news of the patient, she would not voluntarily give any outward token of the torture she was suffering.

John visited every day the hospital where Harry had been taken, and he alone could give the details which Nettie was longing to hear.

At first she listened with coldness and assumed indifference to his accounts; but John was so kind, so tender, so much gentler than she had ever known him, that she could not but break down before it all.

"O John!" she cried one day, throwing herself upon his neck, "did you know it was all my fault? And oh! please tell me if there is any hope."

"My poor, poor Nettie!" he said, soothing and comforting her in his ungainly way, yet which did her more good than anything she had experienced for months.

"I have been wanting so to talk to you about this, and yet did not like to commence it," he said gently, drawing her to the sofa.

"You know all about it, then—how I gave him that glass?" said Nettie, half relieved.

"Yes," answered her brother slowly; "and if I had not been blind I might have prevented it all by one warning to you."

"Oh! I would not have listened to you, most likely; you know Clara and I always called your ideas on that subject 'old-fogy notions'; but indeed I wish, oh! how I wish that I had had the same notions."

"Perhaps this lesson was needed to convince you," said John gently.

"Oh! it need not have been such a hard lesson. Are you sure he will die, John? Just think, it would be my fault— my fault. Isn't there any hope?"

"I am afraid there is very little," answered her brother, not willing to allow her to build on false hopes, and yet hardly able to tell her that there was only one doctor who had the slightest hopes of his recovery.

"There is one thing that is a great comfort," he added: "he is perfectly conscious, and has had a great deal of time for thought during all these long days, and it has not been without profit; indeed, dear sister, we have strong hopes that he is learning to lean on Jesus, and to look upon him as his Saviour and friend."

"Then he will forgive me!" said Nettie more joyfully than she had yet spoken. "O John! will you ask him to-morrow?"

"I don't think it would do to agitate him by going over the circumstances of the accident, but I don't think there is anything he would like so much as a sight of your face; and if mother is willing, I will take you around there to-morrow, for the doctors said it would not hurt him to see his friends, if they did not stay long at a time." He did not tell her that he was considered almost beyond being hurt by anything now, but went on to give her some of his grounds of hopefulness in reference to Harry's conversion.

It was a very awe-struck face that looked down on the sick man's couch the next morning. Her impulse would have been to throw herself down upon her knees and crave forgiveness for being the remote cause of his death; but all excitement had been strictly forbidden, and she could only stroke the one thin, wasted hand that was left to him, and then turn away to hide the tears which would come as she gazed upon that poor marred face.

"Tell her not to weep for me," whispered he to John; "I am better off and happier than I ever was before."

"Have you found 'the peace which passeth all understanding'?" said the other in a low tone.

"Yes; and I have you and Mr. Hervey to thank for it." This was said in broken words which no one could understand but those who had been close attendants at his bedside.

"Would you like her to come to-morrow and read to you?"

"If I am here, I should love it." And Harry closed his eyes, after they had spoken farewell to his sorrow-stricken visitor.

It was some relief to Nettie to find there was the slightest thing she could do for Harry, and John kindly accompanied her the next morning and many mornings after when she went to the hospital to read to Harry.

It made a strong link between the sister and the brother, and the latter could see how this lesson, stern and terrible as it had seemed at first, was working out its own good ends, and might, in time, accomplish what nothing else could have done.

Nettie's remorseful despair was gradually changing to a more healthful repentance, and she was beginning to look at her whole past life with truthful though sorrowful eyes. Her readings from the Book of books were of quite as much benefit to herself as to the one for whom they were specially intended; and as she began to realize from it that there is a Providence watching over us all, she could not but see that the terrible sorrow through which she was passing might indeed be the means of bringing her to the knowledge of Him who alone could save her.

Harry's peaceful resignation to whatever might be in store for him could not but have its effect on her, and at length she was learning to say from her heart what she had long ago learned by rote: 'Thy will, O God! be done.'"

Her conversations with John were a great help to her, now that each had learnted to open the heart to the other.

She had often felt that it would be a comfort to talk of their Cousin Fanny to him, but could never get up her courage to do so, as she had never heard him mention her name since the day of her burial.

One evening, however, he came into her room, carrying a large book which looked like a journal.

"Nettie," he said, turning away his face from the light, "this book was left to me by one very dear, and I think there are some passages in it that may be of great use to you. I can only ask your forgiveness for not having let you read it before; it might have helped you over some hard places."

"Yes; if I had only followed her example!" replied Nettie, knowing well who the "dear one" was; and truly, as she read she could not but pause to contrast her own life with the one partly recorded within its pages.

Especially was she affected by the passages which told of Fanny's joy in having secured a trusty knight-errant, who was going forth on deeds of noble and high emprise. Oh! the gratitude which she seemed to feel when that pledge was signed; and all through the book there was the same unconscious record of good influence which had emanated from her life around upon all those within its circle.

"Could I have but been like her!" thought Nettie; and she gave a sigh of regret as she remembered the far different influence which she herself had wielded. Then came the thought, "Who could tell all that Fanny had passed through before her life had been so purified as to shed around it such a good influence?" Those early days of care and sorrow had found no direct record here, but there was an undercurrent of sadness perceptible in some of these pages which told that the soul, young as it was, had passed through some refining fire.

And should it be for naught that Nettie also was passing through the furnace of affliction—not just the same fire that had tried her cousin's soul, but one, perhaps, even more searching.

Humbly, earnestly she prayed that her life might indeed be rendered fit for a like service. Oh! that she might be allowed to make some amends for all that she had done amiss. But no; even if she lived a perfect life, which would, of course, be impossible, nothing could make mends for the past; but at least forgiveness would be granted her, and she would be helped and strengthened to start out afresh.

It need not be said that her horror of the wine-cup was now equal to what Fanny's had once been, and there was little danger but that in future she would use the whole weight of her influence on the side of total abstinence. She copied some few passages out of the journal, and then returned it to her brother, knowing how he must value it.

"If you would not mind it," she said shyly, "I should like to be able to have a peep at it once in a while, whenever I feel myself growing 'wicked' again or down-hearted about being good."

"Certainly. I have two keys to this upper drawer, and will lend you one, so that you can look at it whenever you feel the need of it. Of course I need not tell you to be very careful of it."

"Indeed I will; and, John, I thank

you so much for letting me see it; it has been such a help to me already."

And so this gentle girl, "being dead, yet speaketh." her life sending forth its influence for good even after her mission on earth seemed ended.

Nettie gathered many ideas from the unobtrusive record of that life. Many embarrassments meet a young girl as she is starting out all untried upon the Christian path, especially when most of her friends are on a far different one. It is hard to form entirely new habits of life, to take a firm stand for the right, when once indifference or opposition would have been the course preferred; but when she found her resolution wavering, one glance into

these pages seemed to encourage her by
the example of one who had succeeded
amid circumstances not altogether different from her own.

CHAPTER XII.

EVERAL months passed by, and Harry Smith was still lingering on in that strange state, hovering, as it were, between life and death. His friends flocked around him, marvelling at the change which had been developing in his character during that time of probation. Once he had been almost a scoffer at religion; now he had learned to look to it for his chief support and strength. Once he would have rebelled at the least necessity for inactivity; now he waited patiently until his time of release should come. He was learning to enter into the spirit of him who wrote:

" Pain's furnace-heat within me quivers,
  God's breath upon the flame doth blow,
And all my heart in anguish shivers
  And trembles at the fiery glow;
And yet I whisper, ' As God will !'
And in his hottest fire—hold still."

After a while a change came; the pain grew less frequent, and there was not so much of that fearful weakness which had so often prostrated him, as it were, on the very border of death.

He had held out so much longer than any one had expected that this change

gave the doctors some hope of his recovery—that is, as far as possession of life
for an indefinite period was concerned.
Health or strength it was not probable
would return to him, but even this was
looked upon as a wonderful triumph of
their skill.

And so Harry was called upon to take
up the burden of life again—for so at
first it seemed to him when he found
that it was vouchsafed to him—not in the
old way, with a healthy, vigorous frame,
but with a poor crippled body and dis-
figured visage. He tried hard not to
rebel—tried not to wish that the grave
had not opened just a little wider for
him; God's strength alone could make

him resigned to what seemed harder than death.

It was his last day at the hospital, and probably this was Nettie's last visit to him; for her parents' dictum had gone forth that these were to be discontinued after Harry was well enough to be re-. moved to his own home.

To Nettie alone did he utter any of the rebellious thoughts which for a time seemed to weigh him down.

"O Nettie! it would have been better if I had died three months ago; I will never be of any use to any one, and just a burden all the rest of my life."

"Harry," she said earnestly, "which do you think knows best—you or God?"

" He, of course ; but then it is hard to see why it could not have been the other way. Just think, I should have been happy now, I hope, and no trouble to any one."

" Don't talk that way, Harry. It must have been for some wise purpose, or else it would not have been so ordered."

"I know that in the bottom of my heart, and you are a real comforter just to say it; and now, you're such a wise little thing, perhaps you can tell me if there is any possible way in which you think I can be of use. You know I really do want to serve God."

"You have done good already," replied Nettie earnestly. " I am sure no one could help being influenced by your patience and submission; and after a while, as you grow stronger, there will be many other ways."

"I am afraid I can never work at all; and if I do get strong enough to write, I shall have to learn how to do it with my left hand."

"There is one thing you can do," said Nettie hopefully; "I suppose a good many of your friends will continue to come to see you, and I am sure you can do good to them. I would get as many of them as will to sign the pledge, and try to lead them to think about higher things than most of them do. I've thought so often, since you were sick, what a frivolous life we young folks used to lead."

"But it will not be so any more as far as you and I are concerned, shall it, Nettie? We can feel that we are together in that, at any rate—in trying to enlist champions in our great cause; and will you pray for me?—for, remember, I have not really been tried yet, and who knows whether I can hold out?"

"O Harry! I need your prayers too; for you don't know how hard it is for a young girl always to stand up for the right. I have been laughed at already for refusing to take a glass of wine; but I don't think all their laughs nor anything else could tempt me to do that now."

"Nor me either—at least I think so now. Who knows what might happen if I were to get really well again? And, Nettie, if that time ever does come, will your mother let such a crippled thing as I am come round in your neighborhood once in a while?"

"You don't need to ask that, Harry; and John will come to see you as often as he can until then."

And thus these two young people were parted, their lives darkened for a while by the effects of what had been partly the fault of both; and yet over all the sorrow of their separation shone the light caused by the fact that, though their paths must needs for the present lie apart, they were, at least, parallel; and even if things were so ordered that they should meet but seldom in this life, that path which each was travelling would, they hoped, lead them to a happy meeting in the world to come.

It was to a very different life that Nettie now applied herself from the one she had pursued before the great event whose effects could never be forgotten. That seemed many, many years ago now, though in reality six months had scarcely elapsed since she had been the thoughtless girl who hardly knew what it was to be sad. And yet, looking back, she could truly say: "It is good for me that I have been in trouble." Though her spirit was subdued, and she felt that what is looked upon as earthly happiness might never now be hers, a sweet peace had entered into her soul which nothing could take from her, and which she would not have exchanged for all the pleasures of that butterfly existence and the many bright dreams which had then been hers.

John was her greatest earthly help at this time; at first each was rather shy of talking on the deeper themes with which their hearts were filled, though the barrier of reserve had for a while been broken down by the events in which they were mutually interested. Their natural dispositions would have led them to retire once more within themselves after life had resumed its usual quiet tenor, but both felt that it would be selfish to do so; John particularly felt that his sister would stand in need of that gentle sympathy which knew how to administer comfort without alluding to the sorrow through which she was still passing.

One evening he found her in his room reading the journal which had become an almost every-day comfort to her. Strange to say, Fanny's name had never been mentioned between them; but now, sitting down beside her, he read a few pages over her shoulder and then said:

"Nettie! it must have helped you to read this; for it seems to me you are growing like her in some of her ways."

"O John! if I could only do the good that she did!"

"There is no reason why you should not try; some of you girls have not any idea what an influence you have over us."

"Not always a good influence," said Nettie, remembering the past.

"A good woman cannot help exerting a good influence, even unconsciously."

"If I could only feel that mine was worth anything now! O John! I really do want to set to work in good earnest. Do you think mother would let me have a class in Sunday-school, as she used to?"

"I will try to get her to consent; and there are a good many things you could help me in, Nettie; if we work together, it will be so much better for both of us."

"O John! that is so nice. You don't know how I have felt these last few days; I could not go back to the old life, and there did not seem to be anything particular to do."

"There will be plenty of that now, and I will introduce you to Mrs. Lambert, her teacher, who was so kind to her; she is just the one to initiate a young girl into active service."

"And," said Nettie, looking down, "there are reasons why I should like particularly to do something in the temperance cause; it seems as if I must."

"Well, you know that is the branch of Christ's work in which I am particularly engaged, so that it seems we are just made to work together. I will give you some pledges, and you can commence to-morrow, if you choose."

"I hardly know any one who I think would sign it," said Nettie despondingly.

"There is no harm in trying; and with such shoals of visitors as you and Clara have there certainly ought to be some. Remember, Nettie, what I told you about woman's influence; you have no idea what you can do until you try."

"Well, I will commence on Charlie and Mary Seton; they are so young, and I won't be afraid to talk to them."

"They are the very ones, then; for an ounce of prevention is so much better than a whole pound of cure. I know some who were in her Sunday-school class who signed the pledge through her influence when they were sixteen, and have never regretted it. It is such a safeguard when they go out into the world; if they feel that they are under promise before they have had the chance to learn to like it, it is so much easier to abstain."

"Charlie Seton is fifteen, and he takes it when he gets the chance; but I think it is more for the sake of appearing manly than because he really likes it."

"That was just the way with me,

Nettie; and if it had not been for our cousin, I feel sure I should have been a confirmed drunkard by this time, for I was learning to love it very much when her influence saved me."

"If I could only be the means of saving some one!"

"Well, try; 'and if at first you don't succeed, try, try, try again.' Do not be discouraged; God is on our side, as I have had to tell myself a great many times."

"And, John," said Nettie, hesitating, "I hope you will stay like you are now. I mean, not shut yourself up in your shell again."

"I know what you mean, sister. I

have blamed myself over and over again for not trying to confide in you, and to gain your confidence long ago, but—"

"No! don't blame yourself. I was not worthy of it then, and perhaps would not have appreciated your efforts; but now I want so much to be like her, and I do so love to hear about her, that if you don't mind it very much—"

So John unlocked his heart, and talked more about Fanny than he had been able to do for many a long day. He told of her visitations among the poor and sick, and what a sweet, gentle influence she had exercised over them for good; but not only among them, for everywhere she went her presence was felt as an improvement, and more than one young man could trace back his first impulse towards a better life to some earnest word of hers.

"And yet, Nettie, she was a weak, delicate girl, not half so well able to go about as you are; so think what you ought to hope to be able to do."

"Perhaps that may have increased her influence with some," replied Nettie.

"That might have been; but, at any rate, I know you will take heart from her example, and not think you can do nothing in the good cause."

"Oh! no, if I can only keep on trying; and it will be such a help to have you to talk to."

"We must strengthen and help each other, Nettie, and I want you to pray for me; for I hope you don't think that I am never tempted to give up. It is discouraging work sometimes, but you will be surprised at the joy which will come with the first-fruits of your labors."

And so Fanny's knight encouraged his sister in entering upon the work in which he himself had been so long engaged. Each had special reasons for activity in the same branch of their Master's service, and it is wonderful what a bond this created between them.

It is beautiful thus to see brother and sister working hand in hand in any great and good cause; and what is there that so unites people as such a mutual sympathy? There were so many things connected with the work that one could do which the other could not, or *vice versa*. Thus the man's strength and independence of movement were aided by the girl's gentleness and winning manners, and John found his success increasing tenfold after his sister began to co-operate with him in his labors.

CHAPTER XIII.

A BITTER LESSON.

ALL these months and the next few years of labor proved to be only the preparation for what was to be Nettie's work in life. Some changes had taken place during this time. Clara was married, and now lived in a distant city. Many of their friends had followed her example, and were scattered here and there over the land; but the event that most affected personally Nettie was that Harry Smith had gradually recovered sufficiently to under take a voyage to California, which the doctors thought would effect a complete restoration to health and strength.

There he was now, and from there he wrote Nettie the letter which told her what she had long known, while she had perfectly understood the honorable motives which had kept him from telling her before.

She would not have hesitated had he asked her six years before to share her life with him, but he had never thought it right to expect her to sacrifice her young life in ministering to him; and so these two had waited on, each apparently free, but embracing no other opportunity which might have presented itself before the one which so happily awaited them. " I seem to have found my mission," he wrote, " and it was discovered accidentally on ship-board; and what do you guess it is, Nettie? No less a one than that of 'temperance lecturer.' I never knew that I had the gift of speaking, but somehow heart and tongue seemed unloosed, and you will be surprised to learn that I have filled several engagements since coming out here, in which the halls were crowded to overflowing. It really seems as if God was giving me some compensation for the loss of my right arm. Enclosed you will find a slip of paper which tells you what the press thinks of me."

And with flushed cheek and sparkling eye Nettie read of the great success which was attending the lectures of Mr. H. Smith—the triumph which she felt atoned for all those years of waiting; and then came the thought of what it would be to become, as it were, his right arm—to join her efforts with his in the great cause he had entered heart and soul.

How thankful she felt that her past labors as her brother's coadjutor had in a measure prepared her for what would, in all probability, be her life work.

To be his amanuensis, to help him in collecting facts and materials for his lectures, and, above all, to follow up any impression which they might hear of his audience receiving by her timely visits and womanly advice—this would be her part in the work, and she could not be too thankful that she would be allowed to take such a share in it.

Harry remained several months in California, and then returned home by land, delivering several lectures on his route; but he was too impatient to reach home to linger very long, and so the wedding was consummated just as soon as Nettie's preparations were finished.

It was not at all the grand affair that Matilda's and Clara's had been. This last couple had been through too much to have any thought for display, and their preparations were in strict accordance with the life which would henceforth be theirs. Harry's father had settled a comfortable annuity upon him; so that he need not depend on the proceeds of his lectures for a support, but intended devoting anything that was left over from them to furthering the great cause.

Their home would be in Cincinnati, as being more central than their native city, and from there they would go on the lecturing tours, in which each would have a work to do, in the manner we have before described. Nettie had a great deal of energy and nerve, and was just the one for the position; and the heart and soul of both were so in the work that few of their friends had any doubt of their success.

John missed them grievously after the good-bys were all said and they found themselves fairly starting together on the journey of life.

Nettie had been so much with him, and had been such a help and comfort for the last six years, that it would seem hard to take up again his labor of love without her womanly counsel and assistance. Soon, too, another "link was to be loosed," another dear life parted from him, and that one he over whom he had watched so constantly, so faithfully for so many years past. His father's health had been failing for some time past, and after Nettie's departure it seemed to decline still more rapidly. Not many

months had elapsed before the latter received a telegraphic despatch summoning
her to his dying bedside.

We must needs draw a veil over the
last moments of the man who could
hardly have been said to have reformed
entirely from the habit which had wound
itself so closely around him. Only his
son's constancy and vigilance had prevented him from falling into the lowest
depths of drunkenness; and though he
earnestly lamented his own weakness, he
had never succeeded in curing it to the
very root.

That life contained its own lesson for
young and old, had any one traced to
its source the habit which had proved

so fatal to his usefulness. In early youth
he had been entirely free from intemperance, but after many years had been
induced to join a club, and from that
time the taste for liquor had grown upon
him. No meal was considered well served
at the elegant house which they had engaged without an ample allowance of
wines and liquors of the finest brands.
No one was considered *comme il faut*
who scrupled to indulge in these to an
unlimited extent; and so Mr. Lodor's club-
life had proved the very bane of his existence.

Let no one think himself safe to indulge in " moderate drinking " even after
middle age has come on with its supposed

accompaniment of steadiness. When the temptations of youth have been safely passed, then it is that the dangers of a supposed security are to be avoided. There are many who have yielded to the temptation from trusting too much to this untrustworthy security; let all, then, young and old, be on their guard, and think not that there is any time of life when the vigilance of their watching may be relaxed.

And now came the breaking up of the home; for it was decided that Mrs. Lodor should accept her daughter Clara's invitation to come and spend a year with her, while John would board in the city until his father's estate had been settled; and

then—well, his plans were very indefinite
for the future, but something within him
bade him go forth and labor in that harvest which was so plenteous and for which
the laborers were so few. He knew not
as yet how it could be accomplished, but
some way would be opened by which he
might be a more constant laborer in the
cause than he had hitherto been.

Not yet had the romance taken flight
from his character, and even yet he did
not feel too old to start out in search of
deeds of "noble, high emprise." Fanny's
Testament still kept its place, and was
well worn now with the constant readings
it had received, but nothing could have
induced John to replace it with a newer

or more substantial one. Old memories still clung around this one, mellowing and softening as the years rolled by, yet losing none of their influence over him whose whole tone of life had been elevated and purified thereby.

There was something particularly fascinating in the idea of starting out as if he had in reality been a knight-errant of old, and seeking to do something towards the improvement of mankind. "The world was all before him where to choose," and he would endeavor so to order his footsteps as to go where there was the most need of laborers in the particular department in which he felt his mission to lie.

But first he must see his mother safely

housed under Clara's roof, and then return for a while to give some attention to those business details which were rather irksome to him.

It was his first visit to his sister since her marriage ; and as he had never seen much of her husband, Mr. Carrington, he felt glad of this opportunity of becoming more intimately acquainted with him. His impression of him was of a pleasant, conversable gentleman, intelligent and well informed, but further than this he knew very little, except that he was engaged in a lucrative business in P——.

Clara met them with affectionate cordiality, and regretted not being able to be with them during the last week or two; but her dear little boy, not quite a month old, was her only and quite sufficient excuse.

"You must be very tired after your dreadfully long journey; but dinner will soon be ready, and I know you would rather wash some of the dust off than do anything else just now."

"If I could just have a cup of tea before I go up!" said Mrs. Lodor, who was feeling very weak and miserable.

"Certainly, dear mother." And Clara bustled out and soon returned with a waiter containing tea, bread, and butter, and, what John saw before any of these, a glass of wine.

"You must drink this to strengthen

you, mother," said Clara, with authority in her voice, but half-subdued by the presence of John, whose opinions she well knew in that regard.

"O Clara! the tea will be a great deal better for me; my head aches so dreadfully, and that is the only thing that ever does it any good." And Mrs. Lodor glanced from one to the other of her children, as if anxious to please both, yet hardly knowing how to do so.

"This is the only thing that ever helps my head." And Clara tossed off the glass of wine herself, glancing with a half-defiant air towards her brother.

John was too much relieved at his mother's safety to worry just then about

Clara. Mrs. Lodor had a tendency of blood to the head without any stimulant, and a very little wine would have been sufficient to upset her. She looked up in surprise as Clara drained the last drop, and then said :

"How can you do it, Clara? I'm sure I could not walk up-stairs if I should take that much wine."

"There is everything in getting used to it, and we will soon get you out of these notions"; she was going to add, "after John goes," but did not express her very obvious thought in words.

John held his peace, though it was a great effort to do so. Clara had thrown down the gauntlet in a very decided manner, but he knew it would not do any good to enter into a discussion while she was indulging such a spirit. She well knew his principles on the subject, so that it was not like hiding his colors to remain silent for a while.

But at dinner-time it was necessary to come out boldly and show which side he was on; for Mr. Carrington, pouring out the wine very freely, pressed him to take a glass after his long journey. John, of course, declined very decidedly, saying that he was a cold-water man. At first he felt almost tempted to leave the table, as it did not seem right to countenance by his presence what he so strongly disapproved of; but then it occurred to him that he might act as a restraint upon the potations of the others. His mother needed all the support he could give her in persisting in her refusal, and if he had not been there it is more than likely she would have at least "sipped a little for sociability's sake."

John determined to have a talk with his sister and her husband before leaving his mother under their care; he knew that stimulating drink would be the very worst thing for her, and, even if they did not think it necessary to deny themselves for the sake of right, they ought, at least, to refrain from the dangerous experiment of pressing it upon another.

Clara was a little startled when she

heard what an effect a small quantity of anything of the kind had on their mother, but she did not say how she had made up her mind before they came that she would be mistress in her own house, and that neither she nor her mother was to be ruled by that old-fogy brother of hers. She promised to yield the point, as far as their mother was concerned.

" But really, John," she added, " I think you would be all the better for some yourself; you look thin and worn out."

" I would probably be still more so had it not been for my temperate habits," replied John ; and a little triumphantly, perhaps, as was natural, he told how in the spring he had pulled through a very severe illness, the doctors telling him that his recovery had been owing, in a great measure, to his years of abstinence both from liquor and tobacco.

"I suppose nothing could have induced you to take a stimulant had they ordered it," said Clara.

"I am very thankful that they did not. I am sure I would not want to purchase my life at such a risk as that would have been. No! if it was given to me to choose, I would say, better a sober, honorable death than a recovery to life and health through means which might have rendered both useless."

"Would you say so in every case?' asked Mr. Carrington, astonished.

" I can only judge for myself, and am very thankful not to have the responsibility of deciding for any one else ; though I would advise every one to seek strength in some other way than in the use of continual stimulants."

" Then what must you think of those who drink it without even the excuse of needing it ?" asked the brother-in-law.

" Oh ! he thinks we are very wicked sinners," said Clara, tossing her head ; " though I really do need it, for you know how weak I get sometimes when I don't happen to get it at the usual time."

" Take care, Clara ; will you not listen to my entreaties ? If I could only induce you to give it up! You know not what it may lead to; it is terrible to think of. Your health does not really require it now, and now seems the time to commence." Then, as Clara shook her head, he continued: "Will you promise at least to limit yourself?—for unless you do—"

"You think I will turn into a drunkard. I suppose," answered Clara, trying to appear insulted, though her brother's earnest pleading had been too gentle to cause real offence.

Mr. Carrington started up indignantly as if to defend his wife; but John laid his hand on his arm in a brotherly way which mollified him at once, and said:

" If you only knew all that I do on this subject, you would not be surprised at what you call my strictness. There have been thousands of cases of confirmed drunkenness among those who commenced as ' moderate drinkers '; many of these took it at first for their health, some even against their will, their principles being overruled for the sake of returning health."

" They must have had it in them to be drunkards; and I am sure I have not the slightest tendency that way," said Clara.

" You do not feel so now, perhaps; but tell me honestly, Clara, do you not take more now than you did at first? Is not the dose steadily increasing ? "

" Of course I am getting more used to

it, and it takes more to do me any good than it did at first."

"Then where is it to stop? O Clara! do, *do* promise me that, if you will not leave it off altogether, you will limit yourself to a small quantity."

"Theodore and I will talk it over together," said Clara, who could hardly help being affected to some extent· by her brother's earnestness. John felt that even this concession was a good deal to have gained, and he determined to take the first opportunity of conversing with the husband alone, feeling that he would be more amenable to reason than his sister; and there were many interesting facts which he knew from his own personal intercourse with those who had fallen into intemperate habits.

Mr. Carrington was indeed astonished when he heard some of these. Could it indeed be possible that women as cultivated, as refined as his wife could possibly lose such control over themselves as to become drunkards? Yes, there was no other name for them after a certain limit was passed, and yet who could define that limit? Was there any danger, could there be any real danger for Clara—her whom he looked upon as almost a model of perfection?

He drew a long breath as he heard of one lovely young wife who had been led into the habit while recovering from a spell of sickness. The doctor had ordered one glass before dinner, but it made her feel "so good" that, for the sake of seeming bright and well when her husband came home in the evening, she repeated the dose before supper on her own responsibility. Gradually the quantity was increased, until there was actually no limit, and then what a wreck was that household!

Mr. Carrington shuddered, and tried to put the thought from him of what it might be if—no, it should not be. He would use his utmost endeavors to induce Clara to give it up; but then could he ask her to do so while he himself continued the practice?

He knew there would be no chance of her yielding to his persuasions unless he himself set the example; and he was not one to stop short at any sacrifice which involved the well-being of one he loved so dearly, and, before they had retired that night, John had the pleasure of signing his name as witness to his brother-in-law's pledge.

It would be a work of greater time to convince Clara, who was more set in her opinions, and more inclined to hold those of her brother John in some contempt.

The effort had not been wholly successful when John was obliged to return, but he had the satisfaction of knowing that something had been yielded, and that the citadel would continue to be stormed until unconditional surrender should ensue. Then, too, he could feel that his mother was safe. Clara's fears on the subject had been sufficiently awakened to cause her to announce the resolution not to take the responsibility of giving wine to any one else, though she professed to have such unlimited faith in herself that she laughed at the idea of danger in her own case.

Her cure was not to be effected without a very mortifying lesson which at length convinced her that, after all, her husband must be in the right.

One day she had taken her usual

quantity before leaving home on a round of morning calls; it was during a holiday season when refreshments were apt to be offered, and so from one house to another she pursued her way, congratulating herself on accomplishing so much, and admiring the open-hearted hospitality of the people. That last glass of wine was particularly exhilarating, and she found herself ready to be amused at the slightest occurrence on the street, and wondered why no one else seemed to think these things as funny as she did.

After a while she noticed people looking at her very intently; the ladies responding to her smile with a broad stare, the boys with a grin, which brought back an answering one to her face. But suddenly she found herself wondering where she was going—in the middle of a broad street with vehicles going hither and thither; and she could not remember whether the car she was to take next was going up or down. A policeman took her by the arm (very gently, to be sure) and moved her out of the way of a cart rattling on towards her; then he was off to duty again, never dreaming of the bewilderment of that stylish-looking woman who had been so nearly run over. She leaned for a moment against the lamppost, and then determinedly walked towards the nearest car, concluding that nothing but exercise would remove that queer feeling from her head and limbs; why was it that the latter would seem to sink under her?

She could have reached the inside of the car, and perhaps recovered herself; but the conductor motioned her back for a moment or so while some of the other passengers got out. One of them jostled her slightly, though it seemed very roughly to her, and in a moment she would have fallen to the ground had not some gentleman caught her in his arms.

"Theodore!" was all she had sense to say as she looked up, and, half to her relief, but somewhat to her dismay, caught sight of her husband's anxious, troubled face.

"Are you sick, darling?"

"Oh! yes; if I could only get home."

"Just come into this drug-store, then, while I run for a carriage." And he half-carried her to a place of safety.

A crowd of small boys, such as ever seem ready to hand when anything is going on, were soon gathered at the two doors of the store to see "that 'ere sick lady." How thankful she felt that the clerks were too busy to notice her, and if she could only hope they would not hear the comments of those awful boys!

"I say, Jack, if she hadn't such a stunner of a bonnet on, I'd say she had a brick in her hat."

"Oh! you go along; big-bugs like her don't never get full of 'stone fence.'"

"No; she's only a little half-seas over," exclaimed another; but all were sent to the right-about by Mr. Carrington, who had come up in time to hear the last remark.

His own vague fears had not dared to form themselves even into a conjecture of any kind, but the scales seemed to fall from his eyes as these words jarred upon his ear, and with a vehement, sweeping kick he dispersed the boys, and went in to help his wife to the carriage, feeling as if a leaden weight had fallen upon his heart.

Not a word was spoken on that most sorrowful of drives. The husband shut his teeth tight together, as if afraid some words might escape for which he might afterwards be sorry.

Clara was sufficiently herself to feel the utmost intensity of mortification. She drew her veil down and sobbed in a way which would have melted her husband at once, had it not been so very maudlin. For the first time a feeling of repugnance came over him towards the one whom he had loved so devotedly. Could this really be she, or was it some frightful dream? But no; their home was reached, and their little boy, now nearly two years old, came running out to meet "mamma." His father thrust him grimly to one side, telling him, "Your mother is sick," and then led her up to her room, shut the door, and left her.

With a cry of anguish Clara threw

herself on the bed, and gave herself up for a while to her grief. To be so degraded in her husband's eyes! Oh! why had she not complied with his long-expressed wishes, and given up that vile, abominable stuff long ago? Never again would she touch a drop of it, if she had to die for it. Oh! would he ever come back and forgive her? Could he ever love her again, after having seen her in such a condition?

These and many other sorrowful thoughts pressed upon her, and it was not till sleep came and refreshed her that she felt at all like herself. Then she arose and washed, changing her dress, and feeling that she could never bear the sight of that violet silk again. A year seemed to have passed since morning, and at least six months since she had seen her husband. Why did he not come and assure her of his forgiveness?

The hours passed on, and still he did not come; but she felt that she could not retire for the night until a reconciliation had been effected. She walked up and down the long parlors, starting at every sound, and sometimes almost resolving to go out and find him. But she would not have known where to go. Their friends were numerous, but he hardly ever went to see any of them without her, and she felt sure he would come in the next minute.

At last she heard his key in the dead-latch, and the door was hardly opened before she was at his side, feeling that they had been parted for an infinite length of time.

The scene which followed is too sacred to be intruded upon by other gaze than theirs. Enough that a perfect reconciliation was soon effected, and it required no persuasion to induce the young wife to sign the pledge of total abstinence, which she most faithfully kept during the remainder of her life.

Need we say that John was overjoyed when he heard the good news?—though, of course, he knew not what had led to it. Mr. Carrington felt that his own conversion to the cause was owing to the influence of his brother-in-law, and he could not but consider it his due to be informed when one still nearer and dearer was brought over to the same side.

And now we must turn for a little while to the affairs of our hero, whom we left nearly two years ago in rather a state of indecision as to what his future course might be.

CHAPTER XIV.

LIFE WORK.

HE settlement of the estate was a much more complicated affair than John had ever dreamed of its being; but, by giving it close attention, he managed to put things in train, so that his mother's and sister's affairs would be in competent hands. Mr. Lodor had made a will, dividing his real estate and bank-stocks among his wife and daughters, while John was to receive a thousand dollars and the interest in the firm of which his father had for many years been a partner, and in which John had been brought up, as it were. The latter would readily be received as a partner, and could have realized a handsome competence therefrom, as they were doing a flourishing business. Judge, then, of the astonishment and chagrin of the other partners when John signified his intention of withdrawing from the firm altogether. They tried to draw from him what his plans were, but he knew he would meet with no sympathy from them, and so went no further into the details than to say he intended to follow the advice of one who thought the rising generation could not do better than "Go West, young man, go West."

"And you'll squander your money out there faster than your poor father could ever make it," said Mr. Bailey, the oldest partner. "That is always the way; as soon as a man dies the money which he has accumulated for his children is scattered to the four winds. Now, just take my advice: stay here among decent, respectable people, and you will make your fortune in less than five years; but go out there, and you'll fall among thieves and come back as poor as a church mouse."

John smiled rather absently; he was thinking about one whose influence over his life had been such that mere earthly riches seemed but a small object compared to that service on which she had sent him. His income would render him independent, and, with no one depending on him for support, why should he toil for that of which he had enough and to spare? Rather would he go out and work in the great field which was white unto harvest, and in which the laborers were so very, very few.

"Come, now," continued Mr. Bailey persuasively, thinking he hesitated, "you've always been a pretty steady young man, and it's a great pity if you should throw yourself into the way of temptation; you'd better settle down here, make a home for yourself, and we'll do as well by you as if you were old Mr. Lodor himself."

Still John firmly declined; he would at least try what he could do in the line which he had marked out for himself, and if it proved a failure—but he could not think he would be totally unsuccessful; he had had a great deal of experience, but longed to exercise his burning zeal in "fresh fields and pastures new."

It was finally agreed that the firm would pay him a certain amount for his interest, in instalments. John knew that it was at a great sacrifice, and that it would have been much better, from a financial point of view, to remain in the firm; but he had no love of money-making for its own sake, and had not the motive for it by which most men excuse themselves for their absorption therein.

It was quite a relief when he had so arranged matters that a fixed income would be his for life; and he could now throw heart and soul into the work which lay before him.

It was a letter he had received from one of his former Sunday-school scholars which had first stirred his heart towards a kind of temperance mission in the West.

This young fellow had followed his father out to some silver mines in Nevada, and from there he wrote a thrilling description of the evils of intemperance which was becoming so wide-spread over the land.

He wound up by saying: "I've tried to

coax some of these men to leave it off;
and if I could talk like you used to to
us, I am sure they would. If there was
only some one here that could gather
them together on Sunday and teach them
like you did us; but every one is bent
on making money, and don't seem ever
to think about the other world. On Sunday some of them go on working and
others play cards and go on sprees. I
hardly know what to do with myself, and
sometimes feel as if I should have to become just like the others. I try to read
that Bible you gave me, and sometimes,
when I get into a quiet place I become
really interested; but I dare not let any
of the other fellows see it.

"Would you please send me some pledges? Some time when they get to thinking of their wives and mothers may be I can find the soft spot and get them to sign it.

"One day some of them wanted me to take a drink; but, of course, I couldn't do it, and then they teased me for the reason, and I showed them that pledge that Miss Fanny got me to sign. They looked at it with wonder; and when I told them how good she was, and that she died not long after that was written, you would not believe how much affected they were; they looked at it with a kind of awe, and not one of that set has ever tried to coax me since. Some of them even look ashamed if I see them drunk, which is very uncommon here, for no one thinks anything of it. I'm sure if somebody like you were out here that they might be taught better."

And this letter had fully accomplished its work of kindling the latent enthusiasm in John's breast.

Those men could not be entirely hope-less cases if a dead girl's name could move them as Fanny's had done. Some "soft spot" they must have, and John trusted to being able to reach it.

And so, armed with his Bible and those pledges, which he hopes some day to have filled up with various names, he starts out on that errand which, in

his heart, he calls " Fanny's mission."
Her Testament still does its work, and it
and the pledge, which is worn almost
threadbare, but which has never been
broken, form the insignia of his office as
her knight-errant.

Not easy is the work which lies before him, and there will be many dis-
couragements on the way; but had these
been sufficient to deter him, he would
have thrown up his labors years ago.
Some portion of success had already been
his, but never until now had he been
able to devote his whole life to the
work

And now will a word be in season
to those of my young readers who have

watched the changes and influences at work in the life of " Fanny's knight"?

All may not, like her, have such extensive influence, but all may do something in the cause which this little book is advocating. Young girls, you know not how powerful is your example; not one among you is without some influence over another. Shall it be, then, that you will not do what good you can by enlisting it on the side of the right? Remember you cannot, without risk to yourself and others, habitually accept the social glass. There are many among you who have given the question no thought, or, if you have, only to laugh at the idea of your example having any weight. But the smallest, humblest of God's creatures must, necessarily, have some influence; will you not decide that yours, whether it be small or whether it be great, shall at least be on the right side of the scale?

And, young men, though you may not feel called upon to give up your life as John did in furthering the great cause of temperance, will you not use such influence as you have on the side of right as he did? You may not feel your danger to be great, but every glass is quaffed not only at your own risk but at that of those who may be influenced by your example.

Pause, then, ere it be too late. If you

have not yet been tempted by the social glass, make up your minds at this present hour that you will resist it whenever it may come; you know not what such a resolution will save you from. If, on the other hand, you have already yielded to a certain extent, hasten to retrace your steps, and may God above give you strength to follow in the footsteps of Fanny's knight!